About the Author

James is twenty years old and lives in London. As well as an author, he is also a published poet. He is passionate about writing stories that illustrate mental health problems in a way that anybody can easily relate to. He was once asked why he writes, to which he replied; 'I don't write because I enjoy it, but because I have no choice; I bleed words.'

Dedication

For mum.

James Shapiro

SUNRISE OVER BELET

AUSTIN MACAULEY PUBLISHERS™

LONDON • CAMBRIDGE • NEW YORK • SHARJAH

A CIP catalogue record for this title is available from the British Library.

ISBN 9781787103405 (Paperback)
ISBN 9781787103412 (E-Book)
www.austinmacauley.com

First Published (2017)
Austin Macauley Publishers Ltd.
25 Canada Square
Canary Wharf
London
E14 5LQ

A heartfelt tale of one man's search for belonging and peace.

Preface

There must be something in the genes because both my brother and my sister have always had an innate desire to run away, to leave society and start afresh, and to find a place they belong.

I myself have never even pondered on the idea of leaving because I have always known that the one thing I would want to escape is the one thing I never can.

'Sunrise Over Belet,' is the tale of how my life would have played out if I wasn't already aware of what I want to escape. It's the story of how I would discover that however far I walk into the distance, I will never truly be free.

One

The first time I ever touched upon the idea of escaping society was in year nine.

It was a rainy, dismal October day and I was sitting in history class staring out the window at a withered magnolia tree. The window was blurred almost opaque from the rain, but I could still see through it. My eyes went back and forth from the teacher to the tree and every time I looked, the window was thicker with rain. There was a fog outside painting the air darker and darker as if night was falling. I could hear the howling of the wind like a wolf at the window, guarding it, keeping me locked inside the false safety of these walls.

Because to me, it felt as though the real storm was stirring inside, not out. The rain falling from the sky just the other side of the window was pure, refreshing, cleansing. The rain in the classroom, however, the rain of words coming from the mouths of a class full of children with social ranks to reach, was poisonous, acidic and lethal. I was desperate to escape.

I tore through the fog and the darkness with my eyes, desperately trying to find the faint image of the magnolia, but I couldn't. All I could see was grey. I felt a panic coming over me; an overwhelming need to climb out of the window and find the tree. I'd fall to my knees on the grass and put my face to the sky, feel the rain and the cold and

I'd feel free. I stared into the now solid coloured window, my pulse beginning to race, each breath filling me with less oxygen than the last, drowning in the rising depths of verbal abuse, filling the classroom like water pouring into a sinking car.

The window had been my only hope. It was a keyhole in a locked door for me to look through into a place I prayed I could be. If I was in hell and the magnolia tree was heaven, then the window must have been the stairs. I wished I could climb them. I wished I could open the window, clamber through it, crawl through the solitude of the storm and bury my face in the mud under the tree, hearing no voices at all, just the falling rain, the whistling of the wind and the weeping of the branches.

A shadow suddenly appeared behind me, followed by a rustling on my side of the window. It was the teacher drawing the blind. He pulled a couple of chords and then it gave. It fell like lead, and it hit the windowpane like a shutter to a vault.

****

Later that day, as herds of school children came pouring into the playground, the clouds began to disappear in the sky and sunlight started to shine down on the school. From the second floor window, I could see the fields in the distance. The grass glistened in the sun and the willow trees blew gently in the breeze. I could almost feel the crisp air, smell the pollen and hear the silence, broken only by birdsong. My body was filling with such peace as I stood on the second floor landing of the stairs, staring out into the distance.

Then it came, just like an earthquake, the stampede of children charging down the stairs, heading for the playground. It was lunch break.

Lunch break to me meant two things.

Firstly, it meant fear. School was a battlefield and everybody seemed to be on the same side, everybody that was, apart from me. I would walk around that prison with my eyes fixed on the floor. Paranoia isn't as it is portrayed in the movies. I didn't constantly look behind me and check corners before I walked round them. I didn't dare look up at all. As long as I kept looking down, no one would catch my eye and I would be all right. Only if I looked at someone and they looked at me at the same time would, I be in trouble. 'If I keep my eyes to the floor, I'll be all right.' That's what I convinced myself. It was my ears that were awake, not my eyes. I relied on my ears to hear if anybody was sneaking up behind me and if anyone was hiding behind the corner waiting for me. Nobody could sense me listening out for them, so I could be discrete as well as being aware. But of course, most of the time, it didn't matter if I knew they were coming or not.

One time, in year eight, I was walking down the corridor alone, my eyes fixed on the tiles that lined the floor of the cooking corridor. I was focusing, without realising, on the lines of the tiles, the grid that ran the corridors length. I was daydreaming about driving an open top car through fields lined with grape bushes, the wind hitting my face and the sun on my skin.

"James, you dirty fucking Nerd." That was a voice coming from behind me, and it jerked my thoughts back to reality so suddenly it made me physically flinch. I recognised the voice; it was deep, husky and overpowering. My flinching was followed by sniggers, telling me of the presence of more than just the one person. I didn't look back, I just kept walking, my legs trembling, my heart beginning to race, my breath quickening. I was scared; the sight of the bush-lined fields were gone and every part of me was back in that corridor, desperate to get to the door at the end which would take me in to the main hallway, a place more densely populated with teachers. 'I might not get hurt today if I make it to that door.'

"James, I'm talking to you, you filthy little teachers' pet." I realised who it was and everything grew stronger; my trembling, my pulse, my breathing. I was done for. His name was Antosh, he was only thirteen at the time but already six foot tall, fully developed, with a body like an ape and a vocabulary consisting of words I'd hate to know where he'd learnt. He was one of those pupils everybody wanted to be seen with and nobody wanted to be on the wrong side of, and he had it in for me in particular. Antosh was the self-proclaimed leader of the biggest gang in year eight.

They say verbal abuse is more harmful than physical abuse. They say it has a longer lasting effect, but I don't think so. I prayed for verbal abuse. I liked it. The longer Antosh and everybody like him spent swearing and threatening me, the less time he would have to spend using me as a punch bag and the less excuses I would have to make to my parents as to why yet another shirt was torn, and why I had been clumsy enough to walk into yet another door. That's the way I saw it, as well as the fact I had been able to grow used to the names and the teasing and hadn't been able to grow used to the pain; I also knew that verbal abuse was far easier to hide.

I wouldn't be so lucky that day. The next thing I knew I felt a smash in my back and my body jerked forward. I felt as though I had left my head behind, my neck ricking completely as my body was thrown forward and to the floor. The door to the safety of the hallway was about thirty feet away. I hadn't made it. I heard my knees clap against the tiles and then a second later, my forehead. I only felt the latter. It was too late to keep my head down and pretend nothing was happening. As soon as I came round from the initial darkness and disorientation, I went to get up. I knew I would have to try to run, something I was dreading having to do because I always told myself that when I know it's time to run, I know it's too late to bother. I put one hand out to push myself up but as soon as I did, it was stamped on. I felt my twelve year old bones crunch and I screeched in pain; however, that was quickly forgotten when I felt something heavy slam into the back of my head, crushing my forehead against the hard tiles. I thought somebody had dropped something on me. It felt like a bowling ball or a brick. I screamed in agony.

The last time I mentioned the bullying to my mum was when I was eight. That was four years before. I had just been punched in the back and I had screamed and cried; cried for the rest of the day and all the way home. My mum had told me that; 'being able to scream or cry tells you that the pain isn't as bad as it seems; it's when you can't that you have something to worry about.' I took that for gospel, but as I lay on those tiles, I felt otherwise.

Another slam into the back of my head, another explosion of agony, another scream, this went on, every five seconds for about a minute. By the end, I could no longer feel the pain in my ricked neck or my back and nothing in my knees. All I could feel was a pounding in the back of my head and that was it.

"Maybe you'll have the decency to look at me when I call you next time," laughed Antosh as he got up off me and walked off, back down the corridor where he had come from, the sound of his footsteps disappearing into the chorus of burning laughter.

This sort of thing happened about once a month, but not a day went by where I didn't have some sort of physical or verbal abuse, usually both. Lessons were filled with name calling, but I knew I was in relative safety providing the teacher stayed in the classroom. I dreaded the end of the lessons, but I couldn't wait for the end of the day. I was in constant contradiction with myself. I spent as much time as possible throughout the course of the day in the classrooms with the teachers, earning me countless nicknames, but as long as I wasn't getting beaten up, I didn't care. Well, I didn't think I cared until years later when the invisible damage the verbal abuse had caused left me in a state far worse than any beating ever had done.

The names they called me and the insults they made me believe were so sharp, I blocked them out and they cut through my skin painlessly, nestling deep down inside. They waited there, dormant, inside me, like unexploded bombs, or fireworks, ready to go off in adulthood.

Lunch break was the worst of the three breaks in the day for the simple fact that it was the longest and also because everybody had it off at the same time, as opposed to the other breaks that fitted around different class timetables. The more time and the more people meant the more pain. It was quite a straightforward equation.

The second thing lunch break meant to me was hunger. By October in year nine, having been back for about forty torturous days, I had only eaten lunch three times. I didn't see it as being unlucky if my lunch money was stolen; I saw it as being lucky if it wasn't. By lunchtime, as the smell from the canteen blew through the corridors, my appetite was at its peak. I almost drooled over the selection on offer that I knew I would rarely get to enjoy. Because of that, I would try to avoid the corridors near the canteen and occupied my mind so that I wouldn't wallow on the reality of it. My mum always told me, 'Nobody pities somebody who asks for it.' So, in order to not be pitiful, I read books, a lot of books, from Charles Dickens to Steven King, from mysteries to autobiographies, from poetry to Economics; I read it all. I would always have at least two books in my bag at any one time, so that if I ever finished one, I would have the next one ready to begin. That way I would never be left in the situation of having nothing to occupy my mind. I would never be left looking pitiful.

So it was the case as I stood there on the second floor landing, looking out at the sun shining onto the distant fields, two big books weighing my bag down with reassurance. I rarely put the bag at my side, however heavy it was; I would take my current book out and put the bag straight back on my back so that I was ready to leave immediately if any threats became apparent. As the ceiling began to shake from the stampede coming out of the classrooms on the floor above and heading straight for the stairs, I was thankful that I exercised this habit. My bag was on my back and it was time to go.

I ran down the stairs, each flight noisier than the last as everybody seemed to charge out of their classrooms at the exact same time. I had been allowed out slightly earlier as I had finished my coursework, something I knew I would regret the next time I saw Antosh who always lagged far behind. I had been in two minds whether to leave the classroom early or not. It wasn't a question of being bullied about it; having finished early, I knew I would be bullied either way, it was just the question of if having a longer lunch break—something that I saw as awful—would be worth possibly getting outside to my corner of the playground behind the shrubbery, before the all-encompassing opposition catches me. I decided it was worth it, and I left the classroom promptly. As I ran down those stairs, desperate to get through the doors to the playground, I regretted pausing on the second floor landing to look out of the window. 'I could have been behind the shrubbery already.' I thought to myself. The shrubbery was somewhere pretty much completely safe because there was a camera on a tree that saw the whole opening. I grew more and more frantic with every landing I passed, and by the time I reached the ground floor, I was almost hyperventilating. Still, I managed to get to the doors before I saw a single person emerge from a classroom. They slammed behind me and I headed straight to safety.

****

There I was, standing alone amongst the leaves, to my right was an ever-growing crowd of people, pushing and shoving each other and shouting and screaming. If I closed my eyes, I could have easily been in a warzone, listening to some sort of genocide. I was in two minds as to whether that would be better than the truth. I knew they were waiting for me to move away from the camera. They never failed to remind me, between the usual insults, that they knew where the camera could and couldn't see. The threshold of my safety was limited to about seven foot square, nestled in the bushes like a trapped animal.

To my left lay a wind worn fence, covered in cracks and holes, and beyond that, freedom. I looked through one of the holes and I could just about see through the brambles on the other side an empty field that seemed to stretch into the horizon. The hole was no bigger than a can and I pressed my face against it so I could see straight through. Then I shifted upwards so that I could no longer see through, but I could smell the air the other side, the free air, the forgetting air, the air with no memory. I closed my eyes against the splintery wood and imagined being out there.

I pulled my face away from the fence, opening my eyes and remembered where I was and what was behind me. I turned around to face it. There was Antosh, in the middle of a huge crowd. He was towering over everyone, even the people in the years above. I could hear all the voices merging into one giant mess of a noise, everybody trying to talk over each other and the chanting and the laughter. It was the laughter I hated most. It was evil. I felt like it was directed at me. I was consumed by it.

Just beyond the playground, I could see the back wall of the history room. The memories of all the names and the insults thrown at me just a few hours earlier whirled around in my head, forming a cocktail of misery in my mind. It was then that I started to think about the magnolia tree, how it blew in the wind, how the rain fell on it so strongly, but so peacefully. That tree summed up my idea of freedom. The fact I couldn't get to it filled me with terror. I felt a shiver come over me. The sound of the blinds falling and slamming down onto the windowpane played over and over in my head. I pictured myself banging on the window, desperately trying to smash through it, but to no avail. Then, as I heard a whistling from the wind coming through the small hole I had just been looking through, the feeling came back, the desperation, the need to escape.

The noise from the playground was growing louder and louder as the crowd grew larger and larger. I felt that same panic I had felt on the stairs coming over me, the racing heart, the breathlessness. I turned and looked at the fence. It was about six feet tall, I was five foot two, I could easily reach the top of it, get a good grip. I knew I'd have the strength to take my bodyweight on my arms. I could hear the whistling, I could sense the sun from the other side as I stood in the fences' shadow. I had to do it. I had to go. I had to go now. The field was calling me, just like the tree.

I reached up and my hands clasped the top of the fence. As I felt its roughness, I suddenly became paranoid that people were looking at me. I remembered the camera and thought about how for the past year and a bit, I had relied on it being reliable; now I was hoping for it not to be. I couldn't hear anything over the noise behind me, but I knew that people were about to start heading towards me. I was breaking the rules, they would have an excuse to at least pull me back in and I would have to face the embarrassment of a failed plan. My stomach became a bag of knots. My breath got caught in my throat. I was at the point of no return.

I put my left foot on the fence and in one motion, propelled my body onto the top of it and immediately leapt over without consideration of what was on the other side.

I fell into the brambles, tearing my trousers and my shirt, and scratching my hands and my shins where my trousers had rolled up on impact. I clambered out and took a small tumble onto the grass. I didn't look back at the fence. I just looked straight out into the open field, feeling the breeze on my body and the sun on my face. The concoction of noise from the other side of the fence was still erupting, I knew everybody had seen me, but I also knew nobody would dare follow me out of the boundary to the school, the kingdom that they ruled. Out here, I was free. The field ahead of me was clear. Looking out into the distance, I could see the rich green of the grass stretching out as far as I could see. It was the most beautiful horizon I had ever seen because it was the image of belonging, something I had spent my entire school life up until that point praying so desperately for; so I ran into it.

Two

As is often the ironic case in life, my troubles in school turned out to be a blessing. Because of the fact I had no social distractions and I spent so much time in the classroom, paired with probably a natural academic flare, I achieved top grades in everything and when it came to further education when I was sixteen, I was offered a place at an extremely prestigious and well-renowned grammar school. By sixth form, my bullying had mellowed, but its effects on my self-confidence had not. I didn't enjoy sixth form; I just kept my head down, accepted it for what it was and got on with my studies. I think I was just grateful that I was finally safe. After achieving three A*'s in Maths, Further Maths and Economics, I was offered a scholarship to study finance at the London School of Economics, something I happily accepted. Three years later, I walked out of that University with a first and a list of companies begging to hire me.

Nothing had pushed me on throughout my A Levels and my degree more than the desire to prove my worth. I had been invisible my entire life, made to feel small and had always been picked on for being weak. I didn't have the body to build huge muscles and I didn't have the confidence to become a fighter, but I did have something; I had a brain. I had a brain that I could use to lead me to a place high up above that school, above the bullies and the abuse they spent their days hurling at me. I had the intellect to become a doctor, a lawyer, a scientist, but I had a point to prove; I had my own position to reach in society, a place where I could sit and look down at the people who made my life a misery and say; 'thank you for sending me to where I am now.' So, with the burning desire to give myself redemption and to empower myself over the part of society I had grown to hate, I became a banker.

****

So there I am, twenty-five years old, in a tailor-made suit, sitting on the platform waiting for the train. To the untrained eye, I had made it. For a while, I would also let myself believe that I had. I'd grafted my way from the bottom to the top and now I was in a position I had always dreamt of being. I told myself the reason I grew up wanting to run away was because I wasn't happy with where I was and I wanted to run to somewhere where I would be; my heart originally lead me to the fields but as I aged, my logic lead me to the city.

I lived in an apartment in St John's Wood, quite near to the station. Monday through to Saturday I would get up at six a.m., leave my house by six fifteen, walk to the station and be on the train by six thirty. I never gave myself enough time to eat breakfast at home; if you work in banking you know to take all the sleep you can get when you can get it. Besides, I wasn't short of a few bob to buy breakfast out every day.

The Jubilee line in rush hour is like the hajj, as huge masses of people pile onto the trains. It baffles me how the trains take so many people, all with their briefcases and umbrellas. You pass Baker Street and hordes of city workers board the train. I think to myself, 'Surely no one else can fit,' but sure enough when the trains stops at Bond Street, even more cram on. You get a moment of solitude at Green Park, which is like the outback compared to most of the stations on the Jubilee line, but all you're thinking about is the dread of Waterloo, when you have to force your body into a shape nobody should be able to go in, in order to let on all the long distance commuters. You have to pre-plan how you are going to go about getting to the door and get off the train about two stops in advance to have any hope of doing so, all whilst guarding your position on the train with your life. It really is survival of the fittest on the underground; and all of that is if you're lucky enough for the train to be running at all.

I worked in Canary Wharf, the heart of the banking world, on the thirty-fifth floor of One Canada Square. I'd arrive at the door of the tower at about seven a.m. and then I'd take the lift to my floor. My desk was in the corner by the window so I had a good view over London. After putting down my briefcase and hanging up my jacket, I would go and get breakfast from the cafeteria before returning to my desk for about seven thirty to start the day's work. My job title was Merger and Acquisition Associate. It was as boring as it sounds.

I was there to explain to managing directors and chief executives of large companies how best to minimize their losses and maximize their profits when they merge or buy and sell other companies. In exchange they would pay my company a small percentage of the value of the deal and my company would split the profits between its employees in the form of bonuses. This small percentage could be in the billions, so I was always generously rewarded for my graft.

For my entire working life, well, all four years of it, I'd been divided. Part of me loved working in finance, I felt like I had made it, I felt powerful. I got to wear fancy suits and go to posh restaurants and meet important people. I quite enjoyed the work as well; I liked the idea that I was having an impact on something much bigger than myself. More than anything, I loved having high up people coming to me for advice.

The other part of me felt empty. I felt like I had betrayed the person I should have become, the dream I should have followed. The problem was, I didn't know who that person was, or what the dream was; I just felt like I was ignoring my true calling.

Growing up, I'd learnt to feel different from everybody else. I don't know if it was because I was bullied or if it was for that reason why I was. I never fitted in and it always bothered me, until I left education and went into the working world and my self-confidence increased. For years then, I had been pleased I was different, because it meant I stood out from the crowd. While everybody was going to lunch, I was working, while everybody was talking sweet nothings, I was working. While everyone was rushing off to the pub at the end of the day, I was working. I was definitely different. What bothered me was that a large part of me thought that I was too different, too different to have the same lifestyle as everybody else. I saw myself as special and it made me question whether I really should pursue such a sensible, solid career, or whether I should instead run away into the sunset like I did in year nine.

****

It was a Tuesday morning and I was standing on the train, briefcase in my left hand, my right clutching a pole to keep my balance. I had caught the unavoidable monthly underground flu and had been coughing for a couple of days. My nose wouldn't stop running. My forehead felt hot and my head felt heavy. My shirt felt too tight and I could feel myself sweating underneath it. The train stopped at Bond Street.

As the hordes of people boarded, the pressure in my head grew and I started breathing heavily, desperate to get to Canary Wharf. Figures were going through my mind; one hundred and fifteen million for Microsoft, two hundred million for Shell, divided by this, times by that. Percentages and proportions, statistics and formulas smashing around in my now pounding head, as the train shook and roared along the tracks before stopping at Green Park. It wasn't like the outback that day, something must have been happening there, huge crowds somehow managed to squeeze onto the already crammed train, pushing and shoving and huffing and puffing. I closed my eyes.

The noise increased in terms of volume but softened in terms of impact. I wasn't bothered by the racket of the shaking of the train or the people, or the announcements, I felt like my ears weren't mine, like I was floating away from my body. I felt safe with my eyes closed, as if nothing could touch me, as if I wasn't really there, only dreaming. My mind started to wander back to my school days, to lunch break, to the shouting and the madness in the playground. I would close my eyes sometimes back then and pretend I wasn't there. It somehow made me feel safer, almost invincible. After all if I wasn't there, nothing could hurt me, and sometimes I almost managed to convince myself I wasn't. I then started to think about that October day in year nine.

My mind took me from the noise of the playground, up that sun-drenched field I'd just clambered into, up onto the horizon to a large willow tree with its almost empty branches swaying in the breeze, causing shadows to dance on the grass below. I had run all the way there and when I got to it, I collapsed to the ground in exhaustion, trying to catch my breath. When it finally came, I crawled over to the trunk and leant against it, resting my head on its light flaking wood. Looking further into the distance, all I could see was green grass, the brown of the tree trunks, the green of the evergreens and the brown, red and orange leaves under every other tree that lay bare in the crisp autumn breeze.

Never had I felt such a sense of solitude, a sense of calm, as if all my worries were meaningless. I was at one with the real world, the natural world, not the world I was forced to accept, the world forced upon me by society. I pictured staying in that field for the rest of my days, growing into an adult and then an old man under that ever-changing willow tree. It didn't fill me with anxiety, it filled me with acceptance. I didn't feel alive or dead, I just felt completely and utterly there. My worries felt so small in the vastness of the land around me that as soon as they entered my mind, they slipped away with the breeze. I sat there, in utter peace. I was in heaven.

Then a dark cloud started to come over and the sky darkened. My worries started to return. It felt as though the stress of life, the reality of my life, was coming *back* to life in my head and I knew I was going to have to face it – to face what I had done. I began to dread going back to school, the image I knew I would have created for myself. I was worried about what the children would think, what the teachers would think and what my parents would think. I couldn't bear the thought of having to get up off the grass and make the long walk back to reality, but as the sun hid behind the grey, I accepted I had no choice. However, I appreciated that I had been able to experience a brief moment of peace, sitting on the grass under the willow tree, while the sun was out.

I heard the train doors opening and I opened my eyes and came back to reality. It was a sudden and mad rush to get off before they closed but I just about made it. Not the field or the tree or the feeling they gave me crossed my mind for a second, as I marched hurriedly up the escalators of Canary Wharf station and out into the glaring smoky sunlight of central London.

****

As darkness came over Canary Wharf and the streetlights came on, I packed up my work, put my overcoat on, picked up my briefcase and left the office. It had been a long and draining day; dealing with arrogant executives who refuse to do anything if it is not precisely their own way. 'They pay good money for my advice just to ignore it.' My brain was whizzing as I descended in the lift and walked to the revolving doors of the tower. As soon as I was through them and the air hit my face, I immediately felt better. The breeze seemed to carry my frustration away with it, revitalising my worn out body as it passed. I knew the London air was polluted, that it was no good for you at all, like breathing in smoke and every breath reminded me. Nonetheless, I still couldn't help breathing it in and kidding myself it was refreshing me.

Sometimes as I walked back from my office to the station, I would let myself pretend, just for a brief moment, that I was standing in the fields under an unpolluted sky breathing in the fresh air. But I'd always quickly stop myself and force myself back into reality before that small thought grew into something more. A car would speed past and the roar of its engine would be the trigger to remind me where I was. I was a banker. I lived and worked in the city. It was my life.

I arrived at the station, went through the barriers and sat down to wait for my train. One positive of the long hours in the finance industry is that by the time you get to go home, rush hour has come and gone and the only people joining you on your commute are your fellow finance workers. However, even though it is nothing like rush hour, it is still enough to fill every train. I watched as the arrival time went from four minutes to three, to two, to one and then as it changed to 'ready' it came into the station.

I got up, picked up my briefcase and stood, waiting for it to stop. It did. The doors opened and I got on, half hoping it would sail straight past St John's Wood and continue into the distance.

Three

I was walking alone, alongside a stream, the sun shining down making the gently flowing water glisten like diamonds as dried leaves crunched under my shoes; a warmth came over me, the sort of warmth that makes your whole body at ease with itself and your surroundings. A family of ducks floated gracefully past with the soft current. I heard countless different birds chirping their own melodies in the trees. A thought suddenly came over me; I couldn't remember for the life of me how I got there. I looked forward and the path I was walking along led on into the sun as far as I could see and when I turned around to look at where I had come from, the end was also beyond the horizon so I had no way of knowing how far I was going to have to walk. I told myself, in a voice that sounded like someone else's, 'As long as I keep following the stream, it will eventually lead me somewhere. It doesn't matter where.' The stream was the only guide I needed. All of a sudden, I heard a slight beeping noise coming from the trees. I looked up at them to see what it was, but I couldn't see anything, just swaying autumn branches half covered in leaves. I carried on walking. Then, another beeping noise, a bit louder this time and I stopped and looked up again, feeling slightly disturbed at such an electronic noise in such a natural place. 'It's just my ears playing tricks on me,' I said to myself and started walking again. The sunlight was beaming down now and I felt soothed and warm. There it was again. I stopped. Again, I scanned the trees for the origin of the noise but I suddenly realised it wasn't coming from the trees; it seemed to be coming from all around me. The sun was still shining on the sparkling stream, but as I looked, with the beeping overwhelming the entire atmosphere, I began to have a sense of sadness. I felt like I was starting to drift away from the peace of the place I was in. I felt an uncontrollable panic spread throughout my body, like I was still anxious about something I had long ago forgotten. The beeping grew louder and louder and louder until the entire place – the stream and the grass and the trees and the sun – began to disappear into a blackening darkness that seemed to spread outward from the deafening beeping. I woke up and slammed my hand down on the alarm clock.

The next thing I knew I was opening my eyes and stretching out in bed. I leant over to see the time. It was ten o'clock. I tore the duvet off and jumped out of bed to get ready for work, where I should have been two hours ago.

****

I sat down at my desk at about five to eleven and was immediately greeted by my boss, Abe.

"Come with me, James," he said and started walking back to his private office. I followed him in. "Close the door," he said, pulling his chair out and sitting down.

Abe crossed his legs and shifted his chair further in, before picking up the telephone on his desk and asking for coffee to be brought. He put the phone back on the hook, clasped his hands and exhaled. I'd been standing at his desk for about a minute and he was yet to say anything to me. He motioned for me to take a seat, so I did.

"Okay James," he began, "we're both professionals. We both know how important time keeping is, so I'm not going to lecture you on that. I know you are fully aware of the importance of arriving on time before trading hours begin." He paused. "You have been doing this long enough to know I am not one to tolerate incompetence from anyone. I run a tight ship here, James, you know that." So far, I thought, he seemed to be telling me everything I apparently already knew. I was wondering when he would get down to the consequences of my 'bad time keeping.' Abe continued. "Now I don't know what you were doing last night, in fact I don't want to know. I'm just telling you to stop anything that will affect your ability to perform in terms of time keeping, in terms of productivity, in terms of everything. Is that understood?" His eyes indicated for me to reply.

"Absolutely, Abe," I said. 'It won't happen again. All it was was…" But he cut me short.

"James."

"Yes."

"I told you I have no interest in why you do what you do, I have no interest in why anybody in this place does what they do, all I care about is that they are doing the things they should be doing and not doing the things they shouldn't. Are you following me?"

"Yes," still annoyed that he had interrupted me.

A knock at the door; it was his PA with a cup of coffee. He signalled for her to come in and put it on his desk, which she promptly did. Then she left, neither of them having exchanged so much as a word.

"Anyway, James", Abe began again, "I know you won't let this happen again."

"No, I won't," I replied on cue.

"Good to hear, off you go. Make up for it," he said, gesturing to the door, before picking up his coffee and taking a long relaxed sip. I got up and walked across the room and just as I put my hand on the handle, he said something so suddenly it startled me. "You've been here four years, James. You're a hard worker. That and that alone is the only reason I'm not punishing you today, so don't be flippant. Next time you're feeling tired when your alarm goes off, just remember that there are a thousand people already awake and eager to take your job."

"I'll bear that in mind," I smiled sheepishly. He didn't.

"Do," Abe replied, abruptly. I opened the door. "Oh and James," he began again.

"Yes Abe," I answered.

"Keep an eye on Eric, won't you?" He noticed I looked puzzled. "Of course, you probably haven't noticed anything. I had a funny conversation with him this morning." I stepped back inside and closed the door, then walked over and sat back down. He continued, "He told me he had been having disturbing dreams recently."

"Oh did he?" I said with lowered eyebrows, sounding more concerned than I had intended. Eric was a close friend from work. I used to be in the same team as him and we had a lot in common. The only difference between us, I thought, was the fact that he was truly content with his city life whereas I was somewhat lying to myself about what I really wanted. But, to everybody else, we were like brothers. We ate our quick lunch together and when we occasionally did join the others in the pub after work, we would always sit together and talk, mostly about work. But through our surface deep talk, we said more than others heard. We spoke silently of how grateful we were to have each other to talk to and of how difficult and lonely our lives had been. He seemed so content with his life however, and I couldn't help but envy that. He told me his goals and ambitions, what department he wanted to be managing in one year, five years, even ten years. He told me his plans, how he'd climb the ladder of our bank and how he wanted to be on the board by the time he was thirty-five. He was twenty-seven then.

"He told me he had been having a recurring dream; something to do with being desperate to leave London, to get away from the city. He said the feeling he had when he woke up was like that of being buried alive. That's what he said. I just listened to him. To be honest, I was thinking to myself that was a bit extreme, but I didn't say anything because a second later, he completely broke down in my office, tears and everything. He looked like a desperate man, James." I looked even more concerned. "Listen, I know he talks to you more than anyone here, so if you notice him acting different, do let me know, okay? I need to know where I am with all my staff. If he needs some time then he can have it. If he continues to be in the state I saw him in today, then it would be best if he wasn't here while he gets over it. So, as I said, if he says anything…"

It was my turn to interrupt. "Did he say anything else to you?" My hands pressing hard against the table.
"Not really James, no; I just didn't expect that sort of thing from a man I have known so long, a man who seemed so content." Neither did I, I thought. "Don't dwell on it. Just get on with your work." I nodded. I knew how much Abe capitalised on my natural tendency to turn to work in times of trouble. "Oh and James, bring your passport tomorrow,

we've got standards popping round to do some security checks." Why was he telling me this now?

"Okay," I said and then left the office.

After I had finally left the office, I went over to my desk and sat down. I picked up a stack of papers to go through and just stared into them as if I'd forgotten how to read. It was fair to say that my mind was elsewhere. 'Maybe I'm not the only one with demons.' I thought, as I forced myself to begin the day.

****

I was leaning back on my chair staring at the digital clock on the wall. It was 'twelve fifty-eight'. Somebody walked past me with a tray of pastries, but I didn't take my eyes off the clock. 'Twelve fifty-nine'. I'd only been here three hours but I didn't have all that much work to do and the day was dragging. I had no client meetings and had finished the stack of paperwork in about half an hour. I continued staring at the clock. Nothing was happening at one, but for same reason I was still eager for the clock to strike it, yet it seemed to be taking much longer than usual. 'One' it said. I sighed and looked away, around the room and back at my tidy desk. 'Perfect.' I'd thought of something, I opened my drawer and pulled out a pack of staples and then picked up the stapler from the corner of the desk and opened it out to refill it. I had no idea what was about to happen.

All of a sudden I heard glass smash as if someone had dropped an entire tray of glasses onto a hard floor. It made me jump and almost staple myself by accident but I managed not to. I put the stapler down and thought about going to find out what had happened. I presumed somebody had dropped something or broken a cabinet so I remained seated. Then, about twenty seconds later I saw two security guards hurtle past me followed by three more, shouting special codes on their walkie-talkies. About twenty seconds after that, there was Abe, running past my desk. He slowed to a hurried walk as he passed and looked at me, shaking his head.

"What is it?" I asked. "What happened?"

"Eric," he replied, and my heart sank. I didn't need to hear anymore; I knew what had happened, but Abe continued anyway, still walking past, turning to look back at me to tell me without having to stop. "He's fucking jumped, James."

I jumped up off my seat and followed Abe through the office, out the doors and down the corridor to the shattered thirty-fifth floor window. There were security guards cornering it off and I could already hear sirens on their way.

"Stand back please," they told us in a cold and blunt manner.

"Shit," said Abe. "Shit. I've got to go and make some phone calls. Are you going to be okay?" He put his arm on my shoulder.

"Yes," I replied. "Go on," and he hurried off.

I walked through a door to the right of the puddle of shattered glass on the floor and into a small stock room, full of printing paper and brown envelopes. I eased a large grey filing cabinet out of the way of a small rusty window and forced it open. I climbed up on top of a box that could just about take my weight and leant uncomfortably against the wall, suddenly noticing the fragility of the building I had spent the last four years of my life in. I peered out and could see the view of London, all the landmarks and the hustle and bustle I had spent my adult life convincing myself that I loved. Then a chill came over me as I looked down at the mangled body of my friend, someone who, I only recently had learned, shared the same demons as me.

Four

John Lennon once said; 'Life is what happens when you're busy making other plans.' He meant that while you're planning what you are going to do with your life, it is passing you by and by the time you realise what you should do, it's too late. I have always had something in me telling me I wasn't happy with what I had, with where I was, with who I was. It's the reason I ran away at school and the reason I always felt in a panic at work and even discontent at home. I had followed a path laid out by my bitterness from my experiences in secondary school, to a place I thought I would be satisfied in being, but I wasn't. As I lay in bed, unable to sleep, looking up into the darkness of my room, I began to finally accept that maybe the path I had followed had been a mistake.

I peered over at my clock; it was four thirty in the morning. I had been asleep but only for a couple of hours. Lying there, I felt completely awake, like I had just woken up from the most amazing and unbroken sleep. My body felt relaxed, but my mind was in a desperate state.

My curtains were for some reason noticeably still. They fell from the railing like sheets of uncarved iron hanging at the wall of a blacksmiths. They appeared solid, almost as if the window had been bricked over. I got up, walked over and opened them, letting in the hundreds of tiny lights flickering from the streets below and in the distance. I closed my eyes and put my forehead against the glass suddenly feeling a sense of tiredness coming over me. Then my eyes opened and my forehead came away from the window and I looked out onto London.

It seemed so peaceful at night. Even though there were still people out and about and the cars were still going past and all the lights were on, it still appeared so calm, so quiet, as if looking out of my window was like looking into a television screen.

My flat was on the seventh floor of an old, solid brick apartment block and I had double-glazing so all that helped keep the noise out. But as I looked out into the city, I felt both physically and mentally apart from it. I knew I didn't belong anymore.

I happily gave in to the tiredness and crawled back into bed and under my duvet, drifting back into solitude before I had time to dread my alarm, my trigger back into the life I knew was nearing its end.

****

Sitting at St John's Wood station, staring at the digital train times with my briefcase at my feet, I couldn't help but feel detached from myself. The arrival time went from five to four to three to two to one and then flashed ready as the train came in to the station. I boarded almost robotically, my body seemed to get up off the chair and walk through the doors of the train without my brain telling it to. My eyes were fixed on the window, looking out into the darkness of the underground flashing by. 'Baker Street, the crowds squeeze on; Bond Street, again, Green Park, a fair few, Westminster, Waterloo, the train is packed and no one can get on; Southwark, London Bridge, Bermondsey, Canada

Water; then at last, Canary Wharf.' I remembered my first day, how as I watched the stations roll by my excitement grew and grew. I felt like I had made it, even though in reality I had just begun, I was at the bottom of the heap but I knew, I thought I knew, exactly where I was going and that empowered me. More than anything, that first day, as Canary Wharf drew nearer, I felt like I belonged. Now, as the train slowed into the station, I felt nothing but emptiness.

It was late March and it had been almost a month since Eric had taken his own life. I'd been just going through the motions ever since, living, working and eating, all without feeling, like I myself had lost the will to live.

I had two things plaguing my mind with anxiety, one being my grief. Eric had been a very good friend to me. I admit he didn't know the real me, but the one I let him know the one I let everyone know, but that is why he was such a good friend. Speaking to him made me feel like I wasn't lying to myself about the life I wanted to live. It reassured me that I was doing the right thing by being a banker and working in the city as opposed to running off into the horizon. I felt as long as he, being someone that knew me better than most, couldn't see through the cracks of my disguise, I was well and truly set to continue living in it.

The other worry playing over and over in my head, the worry which I regret to admit kept me up at night more so than my grief, is the fact I had finally, after all these years, found someone who had the same hidden problem as I had. After Abe had told me about Eric's dreams, even though I was concerned for his wellbeing, I also felt an immediate sense of relief. For some reason, I had always imagined that I was the only one living a life of denial. I couldn't wait till the next time I saw Eric so I could talk to him and tell him he wasn't alone, which I knew would make me feel less alone too, but I never got the chance. The next time I saw him, he lay sprawled out and bloodied on the pavement of Canary Wharf. What did that mean for me? I should have been realistic about the situation and taken solace in the fact that the chances are that if one person has the same demons as me then lots more do too, but as the days rolled past after he jumped, I couldn't help but feel as alone as ever. Like the only other person who shared my hidden problems was gone and I had no one who could understand me. I also feared my own fate, if that was what my worries would lead to. I couldn't sleep at night because I spent my twilight hours desperately praying that there was another way, a way to be happy, but I subconsciously convinced myself that there wasn't, that somehow, Eric knew what he was doing and knew he had no choice.

Exactly one week after his death, I attended his funeral in Windsor, where his family lived. It was a heart-breaking ceremony, but a beautiful one. His family smiled at his memory, through the tears of shock and woe. It was noticeably evident how nobody saw it coming. As they lowered his coffin into the ground, his mother wailed in absolute despair, her husband's arms wrapped around her, tears streaming down his own age worn face. I stood and looked down into the dark rectangular hole as mourners took turns, dropping handfuls of earth onto his grave. Then, just when the person next to me took their handful and I knew I was going to be next, I turned and walked away from the small gathering to leave his family and close friends from home alone with him, and alone with their grief.

I found myself walking into a small opening on the far side of the cemetery. Before me stood an old bench and I couldn't help but be drawn in to its delicately hand carved inscription; 'For John Martins, whose smile could light up a room, so now every time the sun comes out, we will know it's you who's smiling down from heaven.' I pictured this, 'John Martins' smiling and even though I didn't know the man, I couldn't help but wonder if his smile was real or if he wore a mask to cover up his true feelings just like I did. Was I going to take my demons to the grave, or was I going to do something about them? To get into the opening, I had to walk through a couple of light brambles that brushed past my black suit like nature was trying to wipe the misery off my clothes. I remembered stumbling into the opening in secondary school for the first time, feeling like I had finally found a place I could be safe.

The opening was surprisingly grassy considering it was completely hidden under draping trees that, unlike the main cemetery, looked like they had been unmanaged for decades. Just as I stopped to breathe in the fresh, countryside air, I noticed there was a tiny unplanned exit nestled in-between the undergrowth on the other side from where I had come in – about ten feet away. I walked over to it and crawled through, scratching my hands and my suit as I didn't realise how spikey this one was compared to the well-kept cemetery entrance side. A vine wrapped around my left foot as I stumbled out into another, much larger opening surrounded by trees but with no natural roof, just an open sky above but before I could see anything, I tripped and just managed to put my hands down on the damp morning grass. After picking myself up from the ground and yanking my caught foot away from the prickly vine that stretched from the brambles growing in the crevice I

41

had just come from, I looked up and out and let out a sigh of peace.

There was a lake stretching out into the faint distant mist. Its bed of water seemed perfectly still as I looked out at it, but the water that lapped at the crushed stones on the edge of the grassy plane I had stumbled into was anything but still. The tiny wave came in and went out constantly and gracefully, playing the sweetest harmony of moving water I had heard for a long time. From where I stood, with trees lining the outside of the small field, all I could see as I looked into the distance was unbroken, light blue water and bright blue sky.

I walked over to the lake and stood as close as I could to it without getting my shoes wet, so that the lapping water just tapped the front of my shoes. From there I could see either side of the lake, tree lined darkness covered in forgotten undergrowth. But even from my proximity to the water, when I looked straight out into the distance, I still couldn't see beyond the lake. It just reached a point where the mist merged the lake and the sky together as if it went on forever.

Standing in the sun, my body and my mind felt at complete peace. For a few brief minutes, I was so relaxed with myself, that the dread of crawling back through the brambles and getting back to my desperate life didn't even cross my mind. I hadn't felt this free and at peace since I sat with my back resting on the withered willow tree thirteen years earlier. But then, just as it had done back then, the thought came over me like a dark cloud in the sky that staying here forever was not an option and I had to face reality. I hated myself for that thought process stopping me from enjoying the moment while it lasted, but as soon as it came over me, I dropped my eyes from the distant mist to the grass as if I almost felt like I had to stop myself from getting carried away with the idea of staying in this sunlit field forever. But then something happened, something that had never happened before in my life. I lifted my eyes back to the lake as if my brain was overriding itself, telling itself what it should do. The realistic side to me, the side that had led me into my city job and my sensible life seemed to suddenly have no power over me whatsoever. My passionate side, my heartfelt side, my honest side, seemed to take over completely. I looked out into the still blue water and another thought came into my mind, a thought of acceptance of who I was. 'This is me. This is me. This is me.' A voice in my head said and I pondered on what that really meant. It meant that I was finally being honest with myself, at least, I was no longer in denial. I would continue to work at the bank but I could relax somewhat, knowing that that life was nearing its end. I would soon be somewhere else, I told myself, somewhere happy, somewhere peaceful, somewhere where I belonged.

I closed my eyes for a few moments, then turned and walked back to the brambles and without pausing, I crawled through them, then through the small opening and back out towards the others and the bench, into the cemetery where the gathering in the distance was now starting to disperse. I walked along the path and left through the golden arched gates, back towards the station, back towards the life I was beginning to finally accept but for the ironic fact that I knew it was almost over.

****

I thought about that moment as I walked up the escalators of Canary Wharf station out into the flashing lights and buzzing noise of the financial district of the city. Reuter's news and economic data illuminated the sides of the reinforced concrete and grey metal buildings that lined the edges of the small paved square. I looked over at One Canada Square and at the spot where one month earlier, Eric's body had laid in a puddle of his own blood. That spot was now perfectly clean, the paving blocks that were smeared red in the hours that followed his jump were now identical to every other spot on the street, glistening like a sheet of crystal in the polluted glare from the morning sun.

I walked through the doors of the tower and into the lift. About thirty seconds of quiet, just the gentle humming of the lift shaft and then suddenly as the doors opened, I was met by the usual frantic noise of the busy London office.

Work was dragging but I was so separate from myself that I hardly cared. I got through my paperwork robotically as if my body was a machine and I was controlling it with a brain that knew something others didn't. I could see the road that lay ahead of me quite clearly now, as if the fog that had been covering me my entire life had cleared. 'I won't be here much longer,' I told myself, in order to get through the bore of the paperwork stacked high on my desk.

The telephone rang. I picked it up and answered. "James speaking."

"James." The voice said on the other end of the phone, it was deep, slow and monotone and had a certain sadness to it. I knew just by that one word that this person was in a dark place. I wondered why. After a few seconds of silence, they continued, "You knew Eric, yes?" and just like that I knew.

"Yes, yes," I replied quickly. "He was a good friend. What happened is a huge tragedy." I paused. I thought he was going to answer but he didn't so I continued. "May I ask who's speaking?"

"I've got a letter written by Eric," the voice said in a grim, grim tone. "I've got some photos too and a contacts book." Another silent pause. "I want it all gone. I don't want to see them anymore. You were the first name I saw in the book so I just thought I'd call you. I want the stuff gone. I don't feel right chucking it away but I don't care who has it, hence this phone call. I don't know you, James, but if you knew Eric and if he knew you then please come and take his belongings."

For a few moments I didn't know how to respond. Who was this person? They sounded so cold, so low and so bitter. One would easily believe that they had no care at all, but I sensed that they had cared too much and it had broken them. I didn't feel the need to ask any questions. To be honest, a chill came over me and I didn't want to know who they were to him.

"Whereabouts are you?" I asked, taking a pen from a pot on my desk and grabbing a post-it note from the corner.

They told me where they lived and asked if I could come to collect the bits and pieces as soon as possible. I told them I would come that evening when I finished work. They said that was all right and hung up without saying goodbye. I listened to the hum coming from the telephone for a second before putting it back on the hook and ordering my vacant hands to get back to work.

****

I finished work at seven o'clock that night and got on the Jubilee Line to Waterloo and then a train out to Egham, where this person said he lived. It was more or less the same journey I had done three weeks earlier to Eric's funeral in Windsor.

As I sat on the west bound train, staring out of the window at London rolling away into the distance and the concrete gradually turning into countryside, I couldn't help but feel a little bit excited about what was to come. I knew I was making the right decision.

The trolley lady walked past, looking fed up like she was eagerly awaiting the end of her shift. I had never seen a train trolley person in the evening before, but I guessed everywhere was getting busier and it was becoming more in demand. She said to me, "Good evening sir, do you need anything?"

"No, thank you," I replied, "I don't need anything," and I meant it both in terms of coffee and in terms of life. I was soon going to be in a place where I had everything I needed and just the idea of being there was enough to stop me needing anything now. She continued to walk past and I could sense she was holding in a huge sigh of boredom.

The train rolled in to the surprisingly quiet station of Egham. The doors opened and I stepped off the train, hesitating, looking left and then right for the exit before seeing it and walking up the steps and out towards the taxi rank.

****

The taxi driver pulled over at the address I'd told him I'd been given and I paid him twelve pounds and got out, eager and anxious to meet the dark voice on the other end of the phone. After just a few knocks at the door, he opened it. I saw him and almost fainted.

'It was Eric,' I thought. My mind was racing. 'How can this be?' I stared at him as if I'd seen a ghost. I honestly thought I was. 'No. Don't be stupid, I told myself. He must have a twin he never told me about,' and it turned out I was right.

"Come in," he said, his voice sounding exactly like that on the other end of that morning's phone call. He turned and walked inside and I followed him, closing the door behind me and slipping my shoes off in his hallway.

We walked into his lounge and Eric's possessions were already on the table as if this man wanted to get this over and done with as fast as possible.

I stood and looked at the letter and the photos on the table "I presume you're Eric's brother?" I said, half asking, half just making a statement. I had a feeling the man was going to ignore my question as he had done during the phone conversation.

"Yes," he replied bluntly. "Twin." His face cold, his eyes looked weary and empty as if he hadn't seen light for years. "Everything is there," he said. "Please," he gestured to the table, "take it all."

"Are you sure?" I asked him. "It doesn't feel right? Eric was your brother, god rest his soul."

He looked at me as if I was an inanimate object, as if he was looking into a void of darkness, unfocused, just lifeless eyes.

"Take it," he repeated in a single drained tone, and he walked out of the room.

I put the letter, the small pile of photos and the contacts book into my briefcase, taking a glimpse at Eric's photo as I did so. Then I walked out of the room and over to the

47

door, where his brother was waiting. He opened the door as soon as I got within three feet of it. I'd come all this way and I'd only been in his house for about two minutes. I wasn't expecting cake, but a talk would have been something. I looked at him, but he was looking straight at the floor as if he was pretending I wasn't there.

I stepped out onto his doorstep and swapped the briefcase over to my left hand, then put my right hand up to shake his hand and said, 'My name is James, by the way." But without even taking his eyes off the floor, he closed the door in my face.

I didn't move for about five seconds, I just thought about what had just happened. Then I glanced down at my slightly heavier briefcase before walking off down the road I had just come down a few minute earlier. As I took my phone out my jacket pocket to call a taxi, I suddenly regretted not getting the original taxi driver to wait while I made my unexpectedly fleeting visit.

****

Neither the taxi driver nor I had said a word since the original "Hello," when I got in. I'd had to wait about twenty minutes on the street corner for him to arrive. I was tired from spending the day travelling and had a lot of questions going through my mind that I thought I would never get the answer to. Questions such as, 'Why his twin brother seemed so cold? Surely it couldn't just be how he was dealing with the grief?' I also wondered if I really was chosen at random or if Eric's brother had picked me to take his possessions for a reason unbeknown to me. I was waiting till I got on the train to read the letter; I wanted to be able to concentrate fully.

"Tough day?" asked the taxi driver suddenly, with a thick Middle Eastern accent, jerking me back into reality; I think I had almost begun to drift off. I looked over at him but his eyes were fixed on the road ahead.

"Tough month," I answered tiredly, hoping not to get into a conversation.

"What my mother said always to me, when me child, when down," he began in somewhat broken English. "Nobody pities somebody who asks for it."

My ears pricked up and he peered over, taking his eyes off the road for a second, before looking back again. I looked at him and smiled.

"My mum told me the same," I said, sounding almost childlike. "Where are you from?"

"Iraq," he answered, "and you?"

"Just London," I smiled.

"London," he repeated. "The greatest city on earth." I said nothing. "What is business for you in Egham?" he asked.

"I was collecting my friend's things."

"You came from London today?"

"Yes."

"That's good of you, mate." The taxi driver saying mate in his thick accent sounded strange, it sounded forced. "I hope he appreciates it."

"Yes," I replied.

"What's your name?" he asked me.

"James."

"My name is Abdullah," he answered, before he continued, sounding like he was correcting himself, "or Ab."

Then we turned a corner and I saw the station at the top of a small hill. Ab parked in a taxi bay next to it.

"Thank you Ab, how much do I owe you?" I said, getting some loose cash out of the inside pocket of my jacket.

"That's eleven pound sixty," he replied and I gave him twelve pounds and told him not to worry about the change. "You're great man," he beamed.

"What time are you working till tonight?" I asked out of politeness as I opened the door of his car and went to pick up my briefcase.

"Midnight tonight," Ab replied.

"Cor," I said. It was ten thirty then and I felt a late evening chill coming in from the open door.

"But then that's it, James," Ab began, "last day today." A big smile spread across his dark withered face. I knew he was much younger than he looked.

"Last day?" I asked.

"Yes. Then back home, to Iraq – at last."

"Really?" I must have sounded slightly shocked.

"Yes, James. It may be war torn. But it's – it's where I…" he stumbled, looking for the right word. "How do you say in English, it's where I…?"

"Belong,' I answered.

"Belong! Yes, James. It's where I belong; and it doesn't matter where that is, as long as you know," Ab said and sounding like his English had improved throughout the duration of the ride, but maybe he just was talking about something he was passionate about, something that he had learnt the words for. "Where you belong, that is where you have to be."

"You're absolutely right, Ab," I said.

Then I wished him luck, and he returned the wish, I shook his strong, rough hand and then got out of his taxi. I heard a train approaching and I walked through the doors of the station and got my ticket out of my trouser pocket. I couldn't help but crack a small smile to myself as I thought about Ab, this man I had just met, going back to Iraq and then my own life, which was about to drastically change forever. But then my smile straightened as I caught a glimpse of the bold letters on my ticket as it slid into the barrier slot, which read, 'Return.'

****

My head leant against the window of the train as it soared smoothly through rolling fields. I couldn't see anything out of the window other than the odd passing light from a farmhouse glimmering in the distance. I noticed speckles of rain appearing on the window and gradually, there came more and more until after a few minutes had passed, it was streaming down from the top to the bottom, and I could hear it pouring down onto the roof of the almost empty train.

I opened my briefcase, which was lying on the table in front of me, and took out the letter and the photos.

My eyes were immediately drawn to the photos as I put them and the letter down on the table. There were only about a dozen, pictures of him with his family, some with friends and some on his own; he was smiling in every one.

Then I picked up the letter and started to read it. 'Dear Ben,' that must have been Eric's brother. 'If you are reading this then it means I am no longer with you. Don't grieve; I am in a better place. I am writing this in the dark because I can't face the light; I don't want to see the body I pretend is mine. I want to explain to you why I have done what I have done so I can restore my name.' I paused and peered out of the window into the darkness. The rain was

51

getting heavier and heavier. I looked back at the letter and continued, 'I haven't been happy for a long time. The life I want to live is not the life I feel I should live, and I have been living the life I have felt I should be living too long to change to the life I want. I have a demanding job, mortgage repayments to meet, car finance, and bills to pay; but none of that is what is holding me back from changing to the life I know I'd rather have. What's holding me back is the fact that I feel like I would be betraying myself. I have worked so hard to get to where I am and I can't face packing it up, throwing away everything I have spent my life working for. I can't do that. It would make me question my intuition and that is the only thing that is getting me by. I dread what I think is going to happen, how I think this is going to end. I am so convinced I have no other way out that I felt the need to write this so that it is ready for when my time comes. I know you will not understand, Ben. You have a different mind-set to me, you always have done. You are content; I am just a good actor, and I should be, I have spent my life doing it. The only person I know who I think might understand me is my friend from work, James. He has never said anything, but I have always had this inkling that he shares the same demons as me. I see myself in him, but as I said, I am a good actor, a better actor, and he sees nothing in me other than the person I want him to see. I hope to god he discovers the real me and tells me he's the same so that I have somebody to confide in but I know deep down that this will never happen. I have perfected my acting skills so much over the years that I almost believe my own lie.' I felt a tear trickling down my face like the raindrops on the window ten minutes earlier. 'I don't want to die,' it went on, 'but I don't know how much longer I can live like this. That is why I am writing; to explain myself, to apologise for the pain I will have caused. So, I am sorry. God bless and I pray that I see you again one day.' I put the letter back down on the table.

My eyes returned to the dark, outside the rain-covered window. I wished I was in it, drifting away in the rain, floating far into the sky into a place no one could ever find me, a place where I could be alone to grieve and to truly appreciate the insight into my own future that Eric's bravery had given me. But, just like in year nine, my view into the freedom on the other side of the window was obstructed by streams of rain running down the glass. I gave up trying to see through the rain into the distant darkness and rested my head on the corner of my chair and the glass, closing my eyes. My mind relaxed with the gentle rocking of the train as it rolled steadily through the blackness of the countryside.

I must have drifted off because the next thing I knew, the train was slowing down to stop at Waterloo. I rubbed my eyes and got ready to get off, to go back on the underground for what I didn't realise then would be the penultimate time.

Five

I woke up the following morning with my alarm at six a.m.
As I showered and got dressed, memories of the dream I'd
been having that night started to come back to me.

I was in a hellish room – no windows no doors – just
four white walls, a white floor and a white ceiling. I didn't
know where I was or how I'd got there. Lying flat on the
floor, looking up at the white, it was impossible to tell if I
could really see. My clothes were all white and covered
everything. I raised my hands and focused on them as my
body was the only thing of colour in the room, but as I
looked at them, the colour began to seep out, and they
gradually turned white as well.

After what seemed like an eternity, a door appeared on
the wall and I immediately got up and ran over to it. It
wasn't locked so I walked straight through it, but to my
horror, it led to an almost identical white room; the only
difference was that this one had four doors, one on each of
its walls. I dashed to the one opposite the one I had just
come through. It too was unlocked so I opened it and
walked through. Then there I was in yet another room, a
door on each wall. I ran back through both the doors I had
just come through, but when I got to the original room,
three more doors had appeared, one on each wall. The
doors I'd walked through lay ajar behind me, so as I turned
to see where I had come from, I could see the white of the

next room along. After pausing for a moment in disbelief, I headed for the door to the left of me and walked through it. Another identical white four-door room lay before me. I stood for a few moments, entirely lost as to how to escape this disturbing labyrinth. I began to charge desperately through hundreds and hundreds of doors, completely losing my track of where the original room was or how to get back. There was absolutely no way of knowing where I was, with countless doors ajar and many, many more still unopened.

After hurtling through one last door and ending up in yet another identical room, I fell to the floor and put my face in my hands. Things like the need for food and water didn't cross my mind; all I was concerned about was the feeling of being trapped. I wasn't so much worried about dying in here as I was about living in here. A terrifying notion came over me; that however far I walked, I could never escape.

Then at precisely six a.m., I woke up.

I left my house at six fifteen, briefcase in hand and headed for the station.

A poster hung from the window of the station building that had a picture of a man picking fruit with the caption: 'Do what makes you happy.' It was advertising a whisky. I glanced at it as I walked through the doors and scanned through the barriers, before waiting for the train.

Four minutes. Three minutes. Two minutes. One minute. Ready; and there it came, right on time. I got on with the morning crowd and put my briefcase by my feet, as I held onto a bar coming from the ceiling.

I stared into the darkness of the tunnel on the other side of the window, small lights flashing by as the train hurtled along. The usual crowds boarded at Baker Street and I shifted my briefcase closer to me with my right foot to make room for somebody standing on top of me. More came on at Bond Street and then quite a few more at Green Park. As usual, I eagerly awaited Canary Wharf, but I dreaded the day of work. Westminster rolled by and there came even more crowds pushing onto the train.

As it left Westminster station and went back into the black, I looked around at the hundreds of people crammed on to the carriage and then through at the crowds huddled onto the swaying carriage behind. I looked the other way and saw the same in the next carriage along, the noisy inaudible buzzing of countless voices merging into one another and the roaring of the train as if it was going to take off. Looking around I wondered who out of all of these people actually wanted to be here. Hardly anybody was smiling. Everybody was occupied with something, some staring into their phones, others reading books or newspapers, a few doing crossword puzzles. It seemed as though everybody was trying to take their mind off something that was bothering them. Maybe it was the boredom, maybe it was the mad buzz of the crowd surrounding them or maybe, just maybe, it was the tapping of their hidden honest self, knocking at their minds' door. The people that were speaking to each other seemed like their mouths were working automatically, as if they weren't even listening to what each other were saying. Maybe it was just me, but it suddenly felt like everybody had skeletons in their closet, waiting to jump out at them.

I averted my eyes to an advert on the wall above the window, trying to block out all the noise. It was a Christianity advert, trying to get people to join their church. It had a picture of an open field with the slanted script underneath it: 'Don't deny the truth.'

The bustle of the train grew more and more unbearable as it headed towards Waterloo. The volume of the blur of voices grew louder and louder as the train shook more and more as if it was heading straight towards hell itself. The lights flashed in the darkness of the walled tunnel outside the train as it whizzed past. It felt almost as if it wasn't moving anywhere, just staying in one position and shaking madly like it was about to explode. The train slowed as it came into Waterloo, the shaking mellowed, but the noise and the anxiety grew evermore. 'More people are going to get on,' I thought to myself. I didn't know how I was going to tolerate it. 'One more fucking person and I'm going to break.' I almost said out loud. But, I had to stay on, I had to remain standing right in the centre of it; I had to get to canary Wharf and do my job and continue to live the life I had bitterly laid out for myself. I was trapped, I was trapped, I was trapped.

Then, the train stopped at Waterloo, and as the doors opened, I suddenly, almost without realising what I was doing, as if my body was turning against itself for the good of my mind, picked up my briefcase, pushed through the crowd to the open doors that were just beginning to close and stepped off the train.

I paused as the train started to move off behind me, took in a deep breath of air and then just like that, I did something that I hadn't done since the time I climbed over the fence in year nine, as in situations such as that by the brambles behind the bench at Eric's funeral, I knew roughly where I was going to end up. But now, here I was, with a clearing path in front of me, I looked into it, as the train behind me disappeared into the tunnel heading straight to the place society wanted me to be. Then, without knowing where I was heading, I started to walk.

Six

I stood, looking out at the open ocean before me, my mind overwhelmed with peace and the breath-taking emptiness of the horizon. My heart had never felt such solitude, my mind such tranquillity. The water in the distance seemed perfectly still, like a solid plane of glimmering blue, whilst the water forty feet below me lapped ferociously at the sides of the boat. I closed my eyes and felt the chilling sea breeze on my face, the light from the sun shining through the darkness of my eyelids and making me almost able to feel the sight of the golden rays as their heat touched my skin. I took in the noise of the waves below and the occasional seagull squawking in the distance. I consciously listened out to find all the noises there were, but to my utter delight, those were the only two. It was hard to believe that just three hours earlier, I had been shaking with anxiety on that packed Jubilee line train.

****

After I had got off the train at Waterloo, at six thirty in the morning, I'd walked up the escalator, letting my heart guide my feet, rather than my brain. It felt liberating. I knew I was going to get fired. I knew I was going to miss the mortgage repayment on my apartment and I knew I was going to lose my car, and I loved it. I felt such a remarkable sense of freedom, as if all of those obvious consequences were there to highlight and accentuate my feelings of belonging as I walked. With nothing to come home for, I would be truly like the drifting breeze, untied by commitments or my inner governor, which I knew would try to tell me that what I was doing was wrong if and only if I had a reason to come home. But with the knowledge that I would have no job, no home and no car, I smiled at the fact that my inner governor would at long last be obsolete.

I walked into the main hall of Waterloo Station and looked up at the destination boards. As I scanned through all the places and the train times, two people dashed past me, heading towards the barriers. I watched them run through the barrier of platform twelve which was open, with no staff nearby. Then there was an announcement: 'the train to Dover is about to depart from platform twelve.' I looked around at the crowds of people looking up at the train times, the stream of commuters pouring towards the escalators, down to where I had just come from and the huge queues at the ticket machines. The thought of Dover came over me, what it meant, what it symbolised; the port, the sea, the open, everlasting sea.

I suddenly ran through the crowds towards the barrier, straight through it and down the platform to the first doors of the train that were already beeping and about to close. Then, when I was about ten feet from them, they began to close and I hurled myself towards them, feeling like I had my entire life at stake and I threw myself onto the train, not caring if the doors cut me in half as my future, if I missed this opportunity, would be far worse. I jumped, swinging my right arm back to propel me forward as they closed. Then, as I landed on the train, I felt something slip out of my right hand. The doors had closed and I'd caught my balance. I looked through the glass of the door and saw my briefcase lying on the tiled floor of the platform, as the train immediately started moving. As it picked up pace and accelerated smoothly along the long platform of Waterloo Station, I caught a glimpse of the lines that ran alongside the tiles that lined the floor. It reminded me of my year eight cooking corridor, which in turn reminded me of a picture that had lain dormant in my mind for so long, as I lived out a life I had never truly wanted; the vivid picture of grape bush lined fields going into the distance with the sun beaming down onto them, the picture of a vineyard.

Then out of the glass of the door, I saw Waterloo Station disappear from view.

****

The sun, shining through the window of the train, heated my face and it felt as though it was up there in the sky patting me on the back, telling me I was doing the right thing. I knew I was. As we rolled through the hills and the fields, I just stared, with half closed eyes, feeling so unbelievably at peace with myself; I could have easily been asleep without realising it. Then, the next thing I knew, the train was pulling into Dover Station and I realised I must have fallen asleep after all. As I went to pick up my briefcase (before realising there was nothing there) and began to walk to the doors of the nearly stationery train, I couldn't help but feel as though that one hour sleep was the interval between my old life and my new. Would I look back on it in years to come and use it as an indicator to when I finally started to find happiness?

After stepping off the train onto the spartan platform, the first thing I noticed straight ahead of me was the window to the toilets, seemingly not a good first impression of my new life. It was dirty, smeared with condensation; you couldn't see through it even if you tried. I stopped walking and stretched my back from the journey, with the corner of my eye for some reason still on the dirty window. It was then I started to think about that rainy October day in year nine, staring out of the classroom window covered in rain, at the Magnolia Tree, wishing I could be sitting underneath it, free from that school that I despised so much. Back then, I was desperate to escape. I had been my entire life; I just reached a point at around the age of sixteen when I told myself I couldn't. I convinced myself that my future belonged inside the sky-high walls of society, and it was destiny that I was to conform to the pursuit of achieving this pre-decided definition of success. But now, as I stood on that platform, looking back into my past, at my 'childish' dreams, those I had long ago dismissed, I could finally completely accept that it wasn't those dreams that were unrealistic, but my adult dreams which I had foolishly forced upon myself and kept alive for far too long.

After leaving the station, I saw a man in a suit hailing a taxi from the taxi rank. I started to walk over but as the taxi pulled over for him, I stopped. Something inside me was telling me I wanted to be alone on this journey. I wasn't on my way to work, I wasn't going to Eric's funeral or to collect his things, which lay on my bed side cabinet back in my flat; I was on my way to somewhere I had never been before, and I wanted to be alone with my excitement. I saw a bus pull over just thirty feet down the road from the taxi rank and I immediately dashed towards it.

"Does this bus go to the port?" I puffed, one foot on the kerb, the other on the bus.

"It does indeed," said a surprisingly cheerful bus driver, with an old husky voice as if he'd spent his entire life gargling sand.

"Great," I replied and walked on. "How much?"

"£6," he smiled.

"£6?" I asked, eyebrows raised.

"That's English prices for you my boy," he said, "but you're heading to the right place if you don't like English prices."

I smiled and put a five pound note and a one pound coin in his hand and then took my ticket that had just come out of the ticket machine. "I *am* going to the right place," I replied and he smiled, before I walked to a seat by the window and sat down, eager to see the sea. For the first time in a long, long time, I could hardly sit still with excitement.

I had paid £6 for a bus journey that took about fifteen minutes and most of that was spent waiting behind queues of lorries heading to and from the port, although the annoyance of being overcharged slipped out of mind the second I caught a glimpse of the sea behind the trees, as the bus hurtled along the roads between the traffic towards the port. Every few minutes, I caught another glimpse between the trees and the buildings until not long afterwards, the bus pulled over at the stop.

As I stepped out, I could smell the sea air, the salt and the freshness. The breeze coming in was crisp and cold and cut straight through my clothes. I looked out to the open ocean, glistening in the sun. 'This is freedom.' I thought to myself. 'Not a small lake with the other side just behind the horizon, but the ocean, the everlasting ocean.'

There was a huge boat in the port so I walked towards the crowd, messily queuing up to board. A ticket office stood just near to them so I began towards that, but I was quickly nudged on the shoulder by a smartly-dressed and serious-looking official and directed to the passport control office.

For a few terrifying moments, I thought my journey was about to end right there in the port. Then, out of the back of my brain, a memory came to me; Abe telling me to bring my passport in that day. Had I just so happened to leave it in my jacket pocket? 'Please God, let me have left it in my jacket pocket!' I reached my hand inside and felt something hard and rectangular. I pulled it out. I felt my heart skip a beat with relief. I held my passport in my hands.

After sorting everything out as quickly as I could with the passport officers, I returned to the busy queuing area and approached the ticket office where I had been originally heading.

"Where is this boat going?" I asked a middle-aged man with glasses, who was sitting in the office behind a window.

"France," he replied, with no emotion at all in his voice. I guess he had seen too many boats come and go over the years and had never been on one.

'France,' I thought to myself. "France," I said. "I want to buy a ticket, please."

"You want to buy a ticket?" he repeated, almost mockingly with a snide grin stretching across his face.

"Yes," I confirmed, taking no notice.

"I don't know what you think this is, young man," he began, "but that's not how it works. You can't just walk up and buy a boat ticket. This ain't a train station. Booking a ticket on a ferry is a *slightly* longer process."

I looked at him, and in his cold eyes I saw my future fading away. My logic told me to just apply for a ticket and leave when I can, but my heart told me I had to go now and this whole thing was a voyage of my heart, not my logic. "I have to get on this boat," I said, not recognising the sudden confidence that had come over me.

"I've told you," he said sternly, with a projected voice. "That ain't gonna happen."

I had my entire life at stake. My life here was over. I thought about school and how if I had any destiny at all, this was it. Then I thought about Eric and how he had dedicated his life to conforming and making money and had ended up in a bloodied mess on the paving stones of Canary Wharf Square. I knew that was going to be my fate if I didn't leave, and I knew my logic would take over my heart and I would have second thoughts. The longer I put off leaving, the more chance I would have of not leaving at all. Getting on that boat was a matter of life and death.

I looked into his stale old eyes and they looked back at me through his thick glasses. "What if I give you five hundred pounds?" Neither of us said anything, and then I continued. "Right here, right now, then will you get me on this boat?"

"Five hundred pounds?" He smiled in the most patronizing manner I had ever seen. "Lose my job over five hundred pounds?" He looked at me as if he was telling me to go. Then he did. "Get lost mate," he said.

I looked at him in disbelief and it turned into an angry glare, before smashing my fist against the shelf of the booth and turning to walk away. Just as I started I heard him say something from behind me.

"Now maybe if you'd said five *thousand*, I might be a little bit more tempted." I turned round and looked at him again; he was looking back with a sarcastic grin. I said nothing, just thought and then turned round again and walked off.

****

After about two hours of phone calls to banking acquaintances I was hoping I would never have to talk to again, and one bus ride to Barclays in Dover, I came back to the rather surprised looking man sitting in the ticket office and slid precisely five thousand pounds in fifties under the counter.

I have never seen a man so shocked in all my life. He looked like he was going to faint. His eyes met mine again and all of a sudden he went to grab the wad of cash, but I reacted quickly and slammed my hand down on top of it to stop him. He looked at me and I told him the conditions of our agreement with my unwavering eyes. "Okay," he said. "I'll try to get you on that boat."

"Try?" I demanded, keeping my hand pressed firmly down on the money.

"Look, I'm just a ticket man, okay?" His voice almost seemed shaky, his persona all of a sudden, weakened.

"But you know someone who can?" My hand was aching from the pressure I was putting on it. To me, my eyes felt desperate but to him, they must have looked dominating.

"Yes," he said, calmer than before. "Yes, I do."

"Today?" I said, sternly. I noticed the man flinch ever so slightly at my suddenness. It was clear he thought the argument was over.

"Yes, today," he said, looking at me as if I was criminally insane.

"Thank you," I replied, trying not to smile at my own madness. It felt like I had passed the first test of letting my heart rule my head. I almost felt like this was meant to be as it symbolised my road to enlightenment. 'Money had clearly not made me happy, but maybe it could help me on my journey to something that will.' I lifted my hand off the money and slid it under the glass divider, and he shoved it in his pocket immediately, with urgency on a par with that of picking up an asthma pump or an 'Epipen'.

Now, this man, Brian, he later told me his name was, seemed to be a man of his word, because within half an hour I was boarding the boat. All he told me was that 'he had got someone to pull a few strings his end.' I had no idea what that meant, I was hoping nothing too illegal had been done, but to be honest I didn't really care about a man I had just spent five thousand pounds on. I started to think that if I had never become a banker, I would never have had the money to do what I had just done. It is funny how life turns out, but at that point, not a single part of me regretted anything. 'You could have bought a new car.' The voice in my head was screaming at me. But why would I want a new car to drive around the inside of a cage, when I could use that money to escape the cage. As I got onto the ferry, I was so glad I had just done what I'd done. I would have spent my life savings on it if I'd needed to.

"Good luck, James," said my new best friend, Brian, who was walking along the queue with me. "Remember, all you have to do the other end in order to stay out of trouble is apply for"… But my mind drifted off with the ocean breeze. He had written down everything I needed to do, but I couldn't be bothered to listen to his new rich voice, rubbing in the fact that he had my money. Yes, I had no regrets, but I was still a small bit pissed off that this bastard had my hard earned five thousand. My attention was drawn back towards him when he called my name as I stepped onto the boat, sounding as if he had already tried to a couple of times and I hadn't heard. He was standing out of the queue now so that others were trying to board but having to wait for me to walk up the steps.

"Yes," I answered, and looked down from the first step at him standing on the ground about six feet away.

"I hope you don't regret this."

"Don't worry, Brian, I won't." And with those final few words, I turned and climbed the steps up to the doors of the boat, as if I had finally smashed straight through the classroom window.

Seven

One week later;

Happiness is a funny thing. Sometimes it can be something so small that sparks it and propels you to the top of the world, like a walk along a river or waking up from a pleasant dream.

I remember my seventh birthday. I had been looking forward to it all year because my parents had promised me that they would take me to Legoland. I sat in the back of the car driving along the M25 peering out the window at the bright summer sky, watching the Legoland signs roll by, forcing myself to be excited. I had built it up so much in my head for so long that when it finally arrived, I felt all out of excitement. I had a feeling inside me that I wasn't happy and I just couldn't get rid of it however much I tried. The sun shone down as we drove through the gates of the place I had so long dreamed of being in, and I had to paint a smile on my face for the entire day so to not upset my parents.

Compare this to one day when I was around nine. My mum had woken me up for school, primary school and for some reason I just felt so happy, as if everything in my young mind made complete and utter sense. I walked to school that day trying to whistle. My mum was holding my hand and looked at me and said with a loving smile on her face, "You're in a good mood, young man." I just smiled back, *truly* smiled.

I was happier the day before my graduation ceremony, than the day itself. My parents had taken me out for a picnic. I felt like I was slightly too old for that, but I didn't really care. They knew I had got a first and they were proud of me. We didn't go anywhere fancy; in fact, it wasn't even a particularly nice place, just a field near our house, but as we ate our strawberries and our crisps, I felt such an inner happiness. At that point, I thought I was on the right track. It was the time I had the least worries, the least doubts about my future. My dad said, 'I'm proud of you, son;' and my mum told me that she had never doubted me, not for one second. She told me that throughout my troubles at school, she always knew I would make something of myself and find my place. They told me, through smiles and a few tears that whatever I chose to do in life, they would be there for me, as they always had been, every step of the way. They would never stop guiding me; they would never stop loving me.

They both died later that year, my mum in September and my dad at the beginning of December.

I was broken.

The months and years that followed, everything I did seemed to be done out of duty, not out of passion or love. I accepted my job at the bank. I put down the deposit on my apartment. I bought my car. I lived my life, but out of duty. I wanted to make them proud, but I wanted them to see me, to see what I was becoming, what I was doing with my life. Mostly, life seemed like a chore, like I was just going through the motions and waiting till my own time came.

I had never had many friends because I had always, since school, lacked self-esteem and self-confidence, so I didn't have many people to confide in. I bottled everything up, all my feelings, all my woe and all my tears.

As I progressed at work with the natural course, accepting promotions and pay rises, I developed a few friendships, the strongest of which was Eric. Having people to talk to helped me get by until eventually, my grief mellowed enough for me to get back to a relatively normal life.

By the time I was twenty-four, my grief at their untimely passing had worn off enough for me to remember their lives and my time spent with them with a smile instead of the need to cry, and by the time I was twenty-five, even though I remembered them like it was yesterday, it was difficult to imagine what life was like with them around.

I've always found it strange how you can have a feeling inside you, happiness, sadness, joy, regardless of whatever is happening at that point in your life or in the outside world. Why wasn't I happier at my graduation, than at the picnic the day before? Why wasn't I excited on my way to Legoland? Why, oh why was I so at peace that day as my mum walked me to school, a place I had always hated.

It's the same, I think, with peace and belonging. Sometimes you feel it, sometimes you don't and I have never worked out why. All I have ever known is that I wasn't at peace, I didn't belong and I wasn't happy in London, the place where it was my bitterness and misery that guided me, not my passion or my love. But now, I was almost certain, that I was heading to that place. I felt like I was heading in the right direction, even despite the fact I didn't know where it was.

****

I looked up at the light grey sky. The cold and dull atmosphere surrounded me and there was a constant light breeze in the air. I was sitting on the patio of a small wooden shack that had become my new home, on a rocking chair that leant against the wall so that it wouldn't rock. The wooden beams of the patio were damp with morning dew on my slippers and I could see that dew stretching out, away from the decking of my shack onto the small plane of grass and then out into the distance.

An old, slightly slanted signpost stood about six feet tall about fifty feet to the left of the shack, and beyond the signpost lay a dirt track that lead out of view. Even from where I sat I could see the wetness of the signpost, its dark wood soaked even darker.

I leant my head against the hard wooden wall of the shack. It felt solid but somehow very comfortable. I looked across the grass over the gate and out into the emptiness of the distance. Hundreds of symmetrical rows of grape bushes led out as far as the eye could see and I knew they stretched far further still. They ran over the gently sloping landscape in a grid like fashion, painting the land a symmetrical perfection, covering every unwanted mound and flaw the ground had, in a fresh and peaceful pale green. The sky was still a cold and glum grey and I felt my skin gently shivering in the vastness and the chill.

Then on the horizon, a bright orange crack appeared in the grey, its cast caressed my sight with purity and long awaited colour. As it grew larger and spread from the distant sky across the bleakness and towards me, it turned the grey lighter, into an amber then a yellow, before eventually disappearing all together, albeit apart from a bright whiteness above, leaving just a perfect blue all around.

71

The dew on the wooden beams under my feet, the grass and the grape bushes of the vineyard glistened in the early morning sun. As it peacefully evaporated into the sky, my attention drew back to the signpost, which itself was drying in the warmth. From where I sat, all I could see was its slightly rotting wooden back, but from the other side, the dirt track side, one could read what it said: 'Château Belet;'

My home.

****

After the ferry journey across the channel, I sorted out what Brian had told me I needed to do as fast as possible. It took me about an hour to call all the people he'd put on the list and arrange for all the legalities to be taken care of so that I wouldn't get into trouble. After all, I was allowed to be in France, I had just got here the wrong way. Everything was sorted by about two in the afternoon. It's amazing what a bit of money can do if you use it for what it should be used for. I walked to the train station in Calais, hardly looking around me to see the French scenery. I was just desperate to get away from the business and head towards the quiet sanctuary I had in mind when I first saw Dover on the destination board just that morning.

I wasn't sure where to go from there. My sense of adventure had felt somewhat used up and I felt slightly drained and weary. This whole place was new to me. I knew I hadn't arrived at where I needed to be yet but I was uncertain of where that was, of where I should go. I think that it was at that point I felt like I had stopped running away and was beginning to need to head towards it, but I still didn't know where.

I boarded a train called St Jean and paid for a ticket that would take me all the way to Bordeaux with the intention of looking out for anywhere that caught my fancy on the way to make my new home; if I saw somewhere, I would get off and have a look at the area and if I liked it, I would stay. I had enough money to rent somewhere or even stay in a hotel until I found my feet and decided how I was going to earn my keep in my new life.

I looked out of the window of the speeding train as villages rolled by. Nowhere seemed to take my fancy whatsoever; everywhere seemed loud and busy. I wondered how far I would have to travel to find my solitude. To recreate that peace, that sense of belonging I had felt in that field behind my school and that I had longed for ever since. With these thoughts running through my mind and from the exhaustion of the chaotic day, I felt myself uncontrollably drift off into a deep sleep, undisturbed by the gentle rocking of the train, the flickering light outside the window, and not even dreams, just pure, solid sleep and then I woke and my decision had been made for me; I was in Bordeaux.

The low evening sun shone brightly as I got off the train and walked out of the station. The air was still. I got on a bus and when the driver asked me where I was heading, I told him to just to give me a ticket to the final stop so he did, still cheaper than the fifteen minute Dover journey. I kept my eyes open, watching the streets go past, as the sun began to set in the sky. After about half an hour, the bus pulled into the shelter and I got off and started to walk. I had no direction whatsoever; I didn't know where I was or where I was going. 'Is this really what I want?' I thought to myself. 'Why don't I feel free?' In fact, at that stage, all I felt was lost. I heard a large vehicle quite far away, behind me, so I turned and saw it was another bus. I turned back and saw a bus stop about a hundred foot away and without hesitation ran towards it, putting my hand out for the bus to stop. "To the end," I said as I walked on.

After another hour, the bus pulled into a much more out the way looking shelter. Since the start of the journey I hadn't seen a single village, just the odd house or farm. I looked at my watch, it was almost ten at night and I really was in the middle of fucking nowhere. I walked away from the shelter. 'It's warm,' I told myself. 'It's only France – I can sleep rough for just one night.' I continued to walk down roads that seemed to lead me further and further from civilization. Only the odd streetlight lit up the road ahead. I felt like the darkness in front of me represented how lost I felt in my mind. I hadn't even thought about belonging or happiness or the meaning of my voyage for the past couple of hours, instead just finding somewhere to stay the night.

I avoided the roads with no streetlights for as long as I could, but refusing to turn back, I ended up having no choice but to walk down them. It was scary. I hadn't felt such fear since I was a child. The fear of not knowing what was behind me and hardly even being able to see what was in front of me. I used to be able to rely on my ears as I trained them well to listen out for danger in secondary school, but they had long ago stopped being so reliable.

I just walked, one foot in front of the other, feeling out for the pavement in the almost perfect darkness. The occasional car stormed past and its headlights guided me for a very short while but after the car had gone, it felt ever more dark and I felt ever more alone and fearful.

I couldn't see my watch but I felt like I had been walking half the night. 'At least I'd slept throughout the day so it wouldn't be too bad if I was just to walk through the night till morning, providing I'm not run over by one of these cars.' Just as I thought that, a car zoomed past. I hadn't seen one for what felt like a good half an hour so I took my opportunity as its headlights went by and looked around to see get some bearing of I was and where to go.

An old, wind worn signpost stood crookedly on the side of the country road and just before the cars lights sped off into the darkness, I read it. All it said was, Vineyard and hut' with an arrow pointing down a road I couldn't even see to the left.

I felt my way along the side of the lane and towards something that resembled a gate over which I clambered uncomfortably. I brushed my hands along the brambles along the side of this apparent road to make sure I didn't drift off into the woodlands that surrounded me. I kept looking into the distance and felt like my eyes were closing from the surrounding darkness. Then, as the brambles led me round a slight corner, I saw a faint, flickering yellow light in the distance and I headed straight towards it.

As I grew nearer, with every step, it lit up the ground in front of me ever so slightly more. Then, as I clambered through some dense undergrowth towards it, I saw another, bigger light in the distance and started heading towards that.

After climbing over the undergrowth, the ground below me seemed to soften from leaves and mud into something like sand or dirt. As I walked along it towards the lights, I began to just about see the ground in front of me and saw that it was a dirt track leading towards a bushy, grid like field.

I passed by the first light which was on an old rotten wooden shed and headed straight for the big light which was above a large black door on something that looked like an old, mansion house, which itself was also rotting. It was covered in ivy and moss and looked like something out of either a fairy tale or a horror movie. Whatever it looked like, it was hopefully somewhere to stay for the night.

I got to the door and knocked with the big, brass knocker and I waited, and waited. There was no answer. I knocked again and waited; still no answer. I knocked with my knuckles as loud as I could, desperate to get in, but I realised it was hopeless.

Looking at my watch in the light of the door, it was almost one in the morning. I couldn't just sleep on their doorstep, even though it looked like no one was in. What if they were to come back? I presumed whoever lived in this dilapidated and terrifying place wouldn't take too kindly to squatters. So I walked over to the smaller light and felt the wooden wall of the shed down to the ground, which felt like wooden beams. I felt all around to the other side of the shed, opposite to the mansion. This side was less illuminated by the light but I could still see the faint image of a rocking chair leaning against the wooden wall. So I crawled up onto it and sat down, resting my head on the side of the shed. I closed my eyes, but couldn't sleep.

I must have done eventually because the next thing I knew, there were footsteps coming up from in front of me and I opened my eyes to see a large, somewhat intimidating man wearing dungarees, garden gloves and a flat cap. I came round quickly and jolted upright on the chair. Sunlight beamed into my eyes.

"Bonjour," the man said in a thick, heavy voice, his eyes working me out.

"Hello," I said. "Bonjour. Sorry I – I don't speak much – any French. I was lost, I saw this light. I needed somewhere to sleep."

"You are English?" he said, in a thick French accent.

76

"Yes, English," I confirmed, wondering whether or not I should.

"Don't worry, young man," he beamed, a smile stretching across his old, wide face. I smiled back, nervously. "You have been out all night." He spoke in good English for somebody who seemed like he lived in the middle of nowhere. "You poor boy, come with me," he said, holding out his arm to beckon me towards him. "We will go and get you some coffee and some croissants right away." The man seemed so welcoming, almost too welcoming. But I was pleased to be made to feel so at home. I got up and walked towards him and he patted me on the back. It felt like I'd been clapped by a cricket bat. As I walked round to the other side of the shed and towards the mansion, which now looked beautiful in the morning light, I thanked him again and again for his kindness; he just laughed deeply as we walked.

I couldn't help but notice the amazing surroundings that I was so oblivious to the night before. The light morning sun shone down on the grape bushes that spread as far as the eye could see in all directions, apart from the woodland to the right of me. 'I'm on a vineyard,' I kept thinking to myself. 'I'm actually on a vineyard. I just slept on a vineyard.'

Part of me wanted to walk out into the beauty of the fields but part of me wanted to get inside and drink that coffee and eat those croissants; that was the larger part of me to tell the truth. I'd been outside all night. Had I found a place I might belong? Possibly. There was no rush. I was happy to take my time and relax in the mansion for a while.

He went to open the massive black door with an equally massive golden key and as he did he said to me, "Why didn't you knock?"

"I did," I answered.

"Oh," he smirked. "Its common knowledge around here that not even Vesuvius erupting again would wake me up," I smiled as he opened the door and he smiled back. "You've caught on quickly, my boy. You'd feel right at home."

And we walked into the hallway of the mansion.

Eight

"So you're staying then?" That was a voice coming from across the library and I turned to look over, unstartled.

The library was a small room, at least in comparison to the other rooms in the old mansion, but its size certainly didn't make it short of books. The shelves were crammed so tightly you could almost hear the wood creaking, as if everything in the room was about to crack, and countless more books that couldn't fit on the limited shelves were piled high on the coffee table and on the floor in every corner of the room. The library was rather dark, lit only by a big lamp on a stand in the corner and a few odd candles positioned dangerously close to the edges of the shelves so that as many books as possible could be squeezed on. The floor had a thick and furry burgundy rug on top of an equally thick and furry brown carpet.

I had been staying in the guest room in the mansion of Chateau Belet for the past four days and even though I had explored the property, I still found new rooms every day, some hidden behind bookshelves, some behind sheet covered doors. The place only had three bedrooms and two bathrooms but it made up for that with its multitude of living rooms and hallways. There was a huge kitchen, a study, a library, a room for cards and a billiards room. The place was a labyrinth of narrow corridors and stairwells, winding and stretching throughout. One thing that the mansion seemed to lack was windows. There were very few. Only the bedrooms and the main lounge and the kitchen had windows, the rest were walled off. Because of this it was almost impossible for me to know my whereabouts as I walking around the building, as I could never see where I was in relation to the outside world. The house stood an imposing four floors, with a basement, and the stairwells made it difficult to even know what floor I was on but I soon learnt just about. It was a beautiful place and did feel like a homely home, but somewhat eerie; somewhat unwelcoming.

I'd asked to stay for a short while after a long conversation four days earlier, as the owner and I ate croissants and drank coffee in the breakfast room.

****

I'd just spent the night sleeping outside on the rocking chair next to the old shed and even though it had been a very mild night, I was pleased and grateful to be inside. I admired the artwork on the walls of the hallway and the corridor as we walked into kitchen. There were pictures of countryside scenes and vineyards at sunrise and sunset.

After pouring out fresh coffee and putting some croissants in the oven, I was led into the breakfast room, bright from the four yellow ceiling lights, but no windows. "Have a seat," he said, putting his hand out to one of the three single armchairs, which was covered in a green, checkered throw. I sat down.

"Thank you for your hospitality," I said.

"Not at all," he replied, sitting down. "So," he began, grinning, "it's not every day you find someone sleeping outside your shed. What's your story?" I could see he was

80

genuinely interested, a trait I rarely saw in people in London. I'd just met this man. I didn't know who he was or what he had done in his life or even if he would understand me or think that I was a nutcase, but that sincere interest I could see beaming from his eyes, made me feel obliged to tell him everything, so I did.

I told him all about my troubled school life, how I was bullied throughout, how I had always had an innate desire to escape, to run away. I told him all about how I'd never felt as though I'd belonged. He listened intently without so much as a word. I went on to tell him about how I'd felt like the best way to be happy was to get a good career and how I'd achieved top grades in every subject throughout sixth form and university, and how I became an investment banker and had worked in Canary Wharf. I spoke about my apartment and my car and my work colleagues and about my inner demons, constantly begging me to run, to leave the life I'd forced myself into and never come back. Then I told him all about Eric and then finally how I'd, just one day earlier, fled London so suddenly, my briefcase had flung out of my hand onto the platform at Waterloo Station. He sat there looking at me, his mouth slightly open. Before he could say anything, a loud beeping began, like an alarm.

Suddenly, that dream I'd since forgotten came back to me; the one where I was walking along the stream in the sun, breathing in the fresh air and appreciating the peaceful surroundings until an overwhelming beeping started playing, as if it came from all around me in the air. That beeping grew louder and louder until I woke up and realised it was my alarm clock. As I sat in the breakfast room of this old mansion house miles away from anywhere I knew, talking to this welcoming but somewhat strange man about my deepest thoughts, as the beeping grew louder and louder, I had a terrible thought, a terrible, terrible thought. 'What if I'm dreaming?' 'No. This is real. But the stream felt real too. No. I'm going to wake up and I'm going to be back in my apartment, back in St John's Wood, back to my life. My train will be coming within the hour. I need to go to work. No. No.'

"The croissants!" shouted the man, jumping up and running into the kitchen. He had been listening so intently and with such interest, he had completely forgotten about the croissants he had put in the oven.

For a few moments I sat there, taking in all the thoughts running chaotically through my mind. I was so, so happy I wasn't dreaming. When I thought about it in hindsight, I almost smiled at my own foolishness. Of course I wasn't dreaming. You know when you're awake. I was pleased that I'd had this scare however, as it certified my decision in my mind. I thought about how when I looked back on my life, I saw absolutely nothing to go back for. I'd managed to tell my entire life story in about five minutes. That's how you know you haven't been living the life you should have been. I thought about how this man had been listening so deeply that he'd forgotten about the croissants, which must have been burning in the oven.

I got up and started to walk towards the door to go and see if he needed any help, but when I'd got halfway across the room, he came dashing back in.

"Merde! Merde!" he was shouting.

He charged past me to what I thought was a wall decoration – a large rectangular sheet – but when he got to it, he brushed some of it away with his hand and pulled down a handle. He ran through it and I realised it was a door leading to another, even narrower corridor. He ran down the corridor and disappeared behind a door on the right about twenty feet further along. Standing in the middle of the breakfast room, I was unsure of what to do. I just stood and looked down the corridor he'd just run down, waiting. Then, after about ten seconds, he charged back through, carrying a fire extinguisher. He almost barged past me as he dashed back into the kitchen still cursing loudly in French. I followed.

The oven was ablaze; the flames a foot high. I wondered how the smoke alarm had taken so long to go off but then I remembered that I had no idea about anything in this place.

"Stand back!" he shouted at me and I did, as he sprayed the fire violently, white foam falling and piling up all around the oven. Within seconds the fire had gone out, thank god, as most the room, most the house actually, seemed to be made of wood.

For a few seconds we just both stood in silence, him in the middle of the kitchen, me about eight feet behind him, back against the wall. I think he was looking at the blackened croissants lying on the flattened door of the ash-covered oven. The silence was noticeable. Then he turned to look at me and to my surprise his wide smile was back on his face and he opened his mouth to speak, "Croissants anyone?"

I smiled weakly.

****

After cleaning the kitchen and cooking more croissants, we were back in the breakfast room. The coffee tasted fresh and strong and the croissants were delightfully flakey.

"My name is Bernard, by the way," said the man, taking a large and careless bite.

"I'm James. I must tell you, it's a beautiful place you've got."

"Thank you," Bernard replied. "It has been in my family for over three hundred years."

"Why is it called Château Belet?" I asked.

"Château means 'house of' and it's pronounced 'Balay.'"

"Oh, my apologies then," I said.

"Not at all, James," he smiled. "It was the surname of my ten times great grandfather, Geoffrey Belet. The house and the vineyard were passed down to the first born son every generation until my great grandfather who only had one daughter, my grandmother. She married a man named Bernard Abraham and the long line of Belets stopped. But of course, we kept the name for the house for the sake of tradition," Bernard spoke passionately.

"Do you have a wife?" I asked, "A son or daughter?" Bernard looked at me for a second, before replying, "No." He looked as if he was going to say something else, so I didn't say anything. He took a sip of his coffee and then said 'No' again in the exact same tone, almost as if he thought I hadn't heard.

"What's going to happen to the Château?" I asked, wondering whether I should change the subject.

"If I knew that, young James," Bernard began, "I'd be a much happier man." He smiled, unconvincingly, before finishing almost all of his croissant in a few consecutive mouthfuls.

As far as I could see, Bernard was already a happy man. He seemed so content, so at peace. I could see so clearly that he belonged in this place, as if he had no demons, no ghosts, no worries. I envied that. But then, as I thought about how he'd replied to my question about whether he had a family, I reminded myself that I still didn't know him.

"So what are you going to do now?" he asked.

"I've spent my whole life knowing the answer to that, Bernard and it hasn't made me a happy man. Now, for the first time, I can honestly say I have no idea. I have no idea what I'm going to do now. I'm free. Free like the wind."

"I respect that, James. You have given up so much. You must really want to find your place." He smiled, but the smile quickly turned into something more serious and concerned, "But where will you stay?"

"I'll be all right," I replied. "I have a bit of money to keep me going until I find a permanent place to live, somewhere I can live my life without feeling like I want to escape all the time."

"No," said Bernard, sternly, "you will stay here until you find your place," and he jumped up with his plate and coffee cup and patted me hard but affectionately on the shoulder, before walking out of the room with his crockery.

He came back a minute later and sat back down. While he'd been out of the room, I'd been thinking about that very morning when he'd lead me in from the shed and I'd seen the grape bushes sprawling symmetrically into the distance, just like they had done in my childhood dreams. I thought about the open top car and the feeling of the sun and the wind on my face as I drove through the vineyard in my mind. Then my thoughts turned darker as I remembered the lines of the tiles of the cooking corridor and Antosh and classes spent staring out of the window in desperation. Had I found my place? I smiled at Bernard as he sat down and I said, 'Thank you.'

****

85

Later that day after hours spent exploring the house, I finally made it to the door and walked out, down the path and into the vineyard. I hadn't seen Bernard since breakfast; he seemed to have just disappeared into the land and left me to my own devices. He obviously trusted me. The sun beamed down, painting the green of the fields in a layer of glistening gold. Looking out into the vastness, I walked.

The pathways of grape bushes, each one about three feet high, enticed me down them as if there was an invisible force pulling me towards the horizon. I followed them away from the mansion and out into the distance as the sun shone brightly down all around me. I continued walking for about ten minutes, looking only straight ahead into the serenity of the land and nowhere else, not even down at the beautifully rich bushes. By the time I eventually turned back round, the mansion was no more than a faint image in the distant sun.

I spun round with the breeze gently hitting my face and every direction looked the same; not identical, just fabulously similar, every direction that was, apart from the one with the tiny mansion in the distance. I started to walk again away from that direction and out, further into the horizon. Looking down at the pale grass between the lines of grape bushes, a wave of peace came over me. I felt so safe, as if I could duck down and kneel on the grass between the bushes and not be seen by anyone. All I could see was grape bushes stretching out into every horizon. It was liberating to know that even if anybody were to come to me, I would have at least twenty minutes of peace before they arrived. No one could get to me.

I started to run. I seemed to get faster and faster as I flew along the grassy path between the bushes. Never had I felt such an overwhelming energy, as if my body was free and I was drifting almost uncontrollably along the field, just like the breeze.

After a few minutes, still not tired, I slowed to a halt and had another look around. The mansion had now dipped out of view and really the only thing I could see was the vineyard all around me. It was beautiful, it was pure, its simplicity was soul cleansing.

For another half an hour, I walked, at ease with myself, my mind on nothing but the beauty of the landscape and the blue sky. Eventually, I saw some trees in the distance, glimmering in the sun, so I continued to walk towards them. I'd changed direction several times as the pathways between the grape bushes cut in and out of each other in a grid like fashion, so I had completely lost my bearings but I didn't care. It was my garden.

After about fifteen minutes, I arrived at what I saw as the trees; in actual fact, it was an entire woodland that marked the end of the vineyard. One section of the woods stuck deep into the vineyard; that was the part I was entering, whilst the rest of the woods were set about half a mile back, which meant the vineyard sprawled around this side of the woods and from where I was fifteen minutes ago, it gave the impression of being just a small batch of trees in the middle of the grape fields. Now I was here I could see that the woods in the distance marked the edge. As I entered it, I noticed the grass under my feet suddenly turn into flakey and dry dirt. My feet had grown use to the feeling of the grass on the padded soil and it felt like I was now walking on concrete, but after about thirty seconds, they grew use to it. I felt the sun fade away behind the leaves of the trees above me and I walked deeper into the comparative darkness of the woods.

The woods were even vaster than the fields. I spent the next few hours navigating my way through the roughly cut pathways that seemed to lead deeper and deeper into them, until the open fields were nothing more than a distant memory. The trees were quite open, so sunlight still managed to beam down onto the undergrowth. Everything seemed to be so simple here. Where there were grape bushes, there were only grape bushes and where there were trees, there were only trees; the different features in the landscape never appeared to merge.

After quite some time, I decided to start heading back to the mansion.

After much, much more time, I finally found it. The sun was still out, however, as I walked up the path towards the big black door. I still didn't know the way to and from the woods; I seemed to have just stumbled blindly back without knowing where I was going.

The door was ajar when I got to it, so I walked in, leaving it slightly open. I walked across the hallway and down the first corridor and had a peak around both doors at the end, before walking back to the hallway.

"Bernard?" I called out. There was no answer.

Then there was a heavy thudding and I saw the door open and Bernard came in carrying two big sacks. He dumped them down on the wooden floor and looked at me, his arms down by his sides. He let out a big puff.

"James!" he said.

"Hello, Bernard," I replied.

"I was beginning to think you weren't coming back," he said, through thick breathing.

"Here I am," I said, putting my hands out to gesture my presence.

"So you are," Bernard said, smiling. "So you are." We looked at each other for very slightly too long, before he broke the awkwardness. "Where did you get to?"

"I explored the vineyard," I smiled. "It's wonderful."

"It is, isn't it?" laughed Bernard proudly.

"Beautiful day as well," I said.

"I'm guessing you reached the woods?" he said, still smiling, but not as much.

"How did you know?"

"Because you've been gone all day, young James!" he bellowed, almost frightening me. It was as if he was telling the punch line to a joke. I smiled out of duty.

"But James," he said, his smile suddenly turning into a look of serious concern, his eyes fixing on mine, almost as if in terror.

"Yes," I replied, nervously.

"Did you not see the sign?"

"What sign?" I asked, my eyebrows dropping.

"The sign saying 'Do not enter,' James," he barked. I looked at him, quite scared and he continued. "People who go into those woods, James, they don't come out." His eyes stayed locked on mine, his face straight.

"What do you mean?" I said, my voice shaking, knowing exactly what he meant. I felt a chill coming over me.

He continued to stare at me, like he was looking straight into my soul, like I was cursed. Then, just as he looked like he was about to say something terrifying, he burst out laughing.

My eyebrows raised and my mouth opened, I didn't smile, but I felt the chill drift away with a wave of relief.

"You should have seen your face!" he shouted in uncontrollable hysterics.

Then I smiled, but only to keep him happy. To be honest, I was annoyed that he had ruined my peace. But of course I couldn't say anything to upset him. He had been so hospitable. Still, I didn't like the fact that the next time I entered those woods, I would have that joke in the back of my mind.

When his laughter finally subsided he told me to come and take a sack, so I did. Just as I was about to pick it up, he said something else to me.

"Seriously though, James," he said, looking at me with almost as serious a glare as before, "when you did enter the woods and you got past the initial entrance, sticking into my vineyard, which direction did you walk in?"

"I just walked straight," I said, plainly.

"Straight!" he repeated. "You're sure?"

"Yes."

"Not left?" Bernard asked, coldly, and sternly. "Or right?" he said, almost as an afterthought.

"No," I said. "I walked straight. What's left?"

"Nothing," replied Bernard, picking up a sack.

"Bernard," I said, seriously, a little scared again, "what's left?"

"Nothing!" he said with a harsh, raised voice and he walked out the hallway with his sack.

Then, after about five seconds of nothing but the noise of his footsteps as he walked down the corridor, I heard him start whistling, joyously. I stood there for a second, next to the second sack, trying to work Bernard out. He was certainly a complex character. I knew he was hiding something. He'd answered that question in much the same way as that morning, when I asked him if he had a family. What was he hiding? Then, as he walked through the door

90

to the right at the end of the narrow corridor, I picked up the sack and followed him.

****

The days that followed saw me helping Bernard with his chores, helping him tend to the grape bushes on the vineyard and maintaining the land that surrounded the mansion. We ate breakfast, lunch and dinner together every day and we spoke about life, in particular, mine. I told him all about my school days and my work in the city, which bored us both to tears. Mainly, we spoke about the vineyard. He taught me how to look after the land and when and how to harvest the grapes and how to turn them into wine. He told me all about the wine making process and the wine industry and promised that he would one day give me a tour of the barrel house which was just a very short drive away.

I'd only ever known the wine industry from an investment perspective when I worked in banking. I never knew that something so stressful and data driven on the one side, could be so relaxing and so peaceful on the other.

We hardly spoke about Bernard's life. His history remained virtually unknown and his obvious demons still a mystery.

The upcoming harvest was in August. That, I learnt, was when the grapes are at their sweetest, at their best. Bernard told me how every harvest, he hired contract workers to come and pick the grapes, but the rest of the year, it was just him looking after the vineyard on his own.

After three days of talk and getting to know each other, well, Bernard getting to know me, he started to tell me some of his troubles.

"I'm getting too old and weary to look after this place on my own, James," he said in a low and tired voice. We were sitting in the living room. A huge maroon curtain hung over the windows. "My father was sixty when I took over. My grandfather was fifty-five." He was looking down at the floor and only occasionally glancing up at me, as if he was trying his hardest to stay awake. "I'm seventy this year, James. I don't know how much longer I can manage the vineyard." He let out a drained sigh and rubbed his eyes. "I cannot let it fall into ruin."

I looked at him, struggling to keep his eyes open. I felt sorry for him, I really did. He had clearly given his life to this place and he hated the idea of it all being for nothing; of ending his family's long history. He dreaded it, but he saw it as inevitable.

"I understand," was all I could say, deep, deep in thought.

Then, as I continued looking at him, I saw his head droop towards the floor. I thought he was about to cry, but then I heard him breathe in a stuffed whistle and begin to quietly snore.

I sat for a moment, before leaving the room and walking up to the spare bedroom where I had been sleeping, thinking about Bernard and how not even Vesuvius erupting again could distract him from the blaring noise of his demons as he slept.

****

So there I was, sitting in the library, looking up at Bernard who had just come into the room. I had been staying at Belet for four days now. 'So you're staying then?' was what he had said.

I looked at him and then around the room at the books crowded on the cracking shelves, then around and down at the burgundy rugs and to the lamp in the corner.

The light of the lamp reminded me of the sun that shone down so brightly onto the undisturbed field of the vineyard. I thought about how the grape bushes were growing outside as we spoke and how the land seemed so vibrant and alive. I felt a part of it, not like in London where I just felt like another number. I thought about how Bernard had secretly seen me as his successor since he first saw me asleep on the rocking chair outside his shed, and how I had got to know him well enough to realise that he needed me as much as I needed the vineyard. I knew he was waiting for an answer, but I also knew that he was aware of the fact I was deep in thought. It was a stepping stone of my voyage. It was a leap forward away from my old life and well into my new. It would cement my place somewhere my heart had lead me to, somewhere I fell upon accidently; somewhere I belonged. I looked back at the splitting shelves and saw their desperation to escape the boundaries of the screws holding them together. I remembered *my* desperation in school and in work, hidden behind a false smile for far too long.

Then, with the image of sun glistening on the grape bush lined fields in my mind, just like they had done in my dreams, I turned my attention back to Bernard, standing at the door. I smiled and said in a voice so content, I hardly recognised it as my own, "I'm home."

And my smile spread onto his face, and he walked back out of the room, with no more words needing to be said.

Nine

I had been staying at Château Belet for just over two weeks and I already felt more belonging than I ever did in London. In the city, there were a million people doing the same job as me. I upped and left with no notice and I bet I was forgotten within hours. I wasn't needed there, just like a leaf isn't needed for shade on a tree full of leaves, but Belet needed me. In Belet, I wasn't just a leaf among many; I was the trunk, and the land was a person sitting in the shade of my canopy. The land relied on me to look after it as much as I relied on *it* to keep me sane, to give me purpose and to keep me at peace.

Every day I would cut the weeds and plant new grass seeds and walk the fields, making sure everything was okay with the grape bushes, which grew taller and taller. The sun shone down relentlessly dawn till dusk.

I'd eat most of my meals with Bernard, but sometimes he would leave me on my own in the house for whole days at a time when he was, 'Popping into town.' Usually, though, I'd eat, sit and talk with Bernard in the evenings. We'd talk about everything. I felt a strong bond growing between us, as he taught me the art of grape growing and wine making, but more importantly the art of being content.

One day, I mowed the entire vineyard, every pathway that cut through; in all, it must have been miles and miles of land.

Bernard and I were on the patio later that day as the sun set, sitting on separate wooden chairs, looking out into the land. The lines of grape bushes seemed even more perfect with the short grass and the vineyard seemed especially beautiful. We said nothing to each other, just looked out at my work in admiration.

"I'm proud of you, son," I heard Bernard say in a quiet, but sincere voice. I said nothing, just looked over at him and gave a small, thankful smile, before looking back into the vastness of the land and thinking about my dad, then my mum and hoping they weren't looking back at me in disappointment.

****

It was my twenty-sixth birthday and I had been at Belet for almost two months. I didn't intentionally tell Bernard, it must have just come up in passing at some stage, but he had remembered.

We were sitting in one of the smaller living rooms with no windows, but curtains for decorative purposes, maybe to give the impression of windows, hung on one of the walls. The curtains were a dark, rich purple, matching the decorative carpet and the two chairs, which used to be rocking chairs but had long ago broken, were covered in thick dark green cushioned rugs. A little mahogany chest of draws stood next to a small fireplace that crackled in the corner, warming and partially lighting the dim room.

"Here you go, James," said Bernard in a croaky voice, handing me a small neatly wrapped parcel.

"You shouldn't have," I said, smiling, taking the present.

"Nonsense," replied Bernard, beaming across the room at me. "Well, open it up then, my boy." He gestured to the present he'd just handed me with his big, worn hand.

"I will," I said, but I wanted to continue looking at it in its wrapping for a few moments instead. I wanted to savour the moment; I hadn't received a present I cared so much about for five years.

Then I opened it.

It was box and inside the box, a label, folded neatly into quarters. I looked at it and then at Bernard with a puzzled look on my face.

"Turn it round," he said.

I picked the label up gently from the box, being careful not to damage something that I obviously was yet to understand. I looked at it again, trying to work it out.

"It's a label for our wine," I said, half asking, looking back at Bernard, who was still smiling widely.

"Yes. Turn it round," he repeated. So I did.

Then I understood.

'Bernard James.' It had written on it in Old English writing. 'Fine Red Wine from Château Belet, Bordeaux.'

I looked at Bernard, holding the label tight in both hands, a smile starting to spread uncontrollably across my face in disbelief and gratitude. I didn't know what to say.

"I'm sorry I didn't call it James Bernard. I thought about it, but it just didn't have the same ring to it," Bernard said jokingly.

I continued to look at him, still trying to believe that he had named that year's wine after me. Then at almost exactly the same time, we both burst out laughing.

"Bernard James," I said, as the laughter died down to a chuckling. "Bernard James." Then, rather embarrassingly, I began to cry. I suddenly realised just how at home I felt.

How this whole thing was mine. I'd looked after the land and now my name would be on the wine in the upcoming grape harvest. 'Bernard James.' I thought to myself over and over again, 'my name on the bottle.'

Bernard got up and patted me tenderly and lovingly on the shoulder. Then, without saying anything, went to the corner of the room and got a tissue out of the drawer. He brought it back to me and handed it to me and I took it and dabbed my eyes. He stood there for a second looking down at me, as if he saw me as his own family. "Glad you like it, son," he said, and walked slowly out of the room.

"Bernard James," I said quietly to myself. Then sat on my own in silence for most of the rest of the evening, just thinking about where I was, about who I was.

****

The upcoming harvest was in August, which was just over a month's time. It was, I'd been told, the busiest time of year for vineyard workers and wine makers, as it was the time of year that the grapes were picked and pressed into wine. The wine would be sold in huge cases by the thousand. There would be contract staff helping on the vineyard, foreign investors having a look around and lorries coming in and out every hour of every day. It was going to be a huge operation.

Bernard seemed to be letting me take on more and more responsibility every day. At first I thought it was because he wanted me to be fully prepared and ready for the harvest but gradually, as I saw less and less of him on the fields as the days went by, I started to get the feeling that something was wrong.

By the end of July, the grape bushes had grown to such a staggering height I could no longer see over them and into the distance. It gave a different perspective to the land. Everything felt more mysterious, more unknown, every step filled me with slightly more doubt than when I could see the open fields clearly back in the late spring. Still, however, the vineyard was as therapeutic as ever and much more importantly, I still belonged.

I hadn't been back to the woods. The idea of them filled me with slight dread and unease. I felt as though something was hiding in them, almost waiting for me to return. I told myself I was stupid and planned to intentionally go back one of the days to get over my irrational fear, but I always found some excuse not to.

Usually, as I worked alone on the fields, I thought about my life and how the life I was living was all I had ever truly wanted. I knew in my heart that my parents would be proud of me because I was following my calling. I knew they were looking down on me and smiling. The thought of that made me smile. I thought about Eric up in heaven, looking down on me. I wondered if he would be happy for me. I wondered if he would feel as though at least some good came of his suicide, as it had possibly saved my life. I always felt guilty for thinking like that; guilty, but overwhelmingly grateful.

I sometimes closed my eyes, standing in the middle of the vineyard and tried to imagine I was back in high school down the cooking corridor or in history class. I'd picture myself blocking out the racket from the other students and in my mind I would make myself believe that I was there, trying desperately to believe that I was standing in the middle of a vineyard in the sun, free and happy. I would keep my eyes closed tight for a while, taking in the

98

memories of anxiety and desperation and then I'd slowly open my eyes and try to make myself believe that I had teleported to where I was now and that my desperate prayers had been answered.

Often I would think about my bullying and ask myself if that is what led me here, if that is what made me the way I am or if it was because of the way I am that I was bullied in the first place. I couldn't answer my own question and it stressed me out, so I would always try to forget about it and appreciate where I was, finding solace in the fact that it no longer mattered.

If Bernard ever saw me dwelling on my troubled past, he would purposely change the subject. I would sometimes get so caught up in traumatic memories like being beaten up, I'd feel sick and almost throw up or shudder. Bernard would always remind me that I was no longer there. I was safe. He said he would always be there for me.

****

It was the first of August and for the first time in a long time, a few grey clouds came overhead and it began to rain. The idea of it was refreshing, but when I looked out of the window of the main living room, for some reason, it filled me with cold and a sense of hostility. It had been sunny for so long, I had almost forgotten what it was like to see the rain. I use to love it. It use to wash away all my worries as it fell gracefully from the sky, and it would carry them away as it formed streams flowing downhill and into the distance. But looking out of that window, it seemed to do the same to my peace. It seemed to carry away whatever I felt with it, putting me back to my basic self.

"James," I heard Bernard calling me, weakly, from the other living room with the purple wall curtains.

"Coming," I replied and turned away from the window which was becoming more and more blurry in the rain, which seemed to be falling harder and harder.

I walked through the narrow corridor and down an even narrower set of stairs and then through a creaky wooden door and into the other living room. When I got there I saw Bernard sitting on the chair with his eyes closed, breathing lightly.

"I'm here, Bernard," I said quietly, trying not to startle him.

"James," he said, very quietly, so I could just about hear. He seemed so weak and tired. I thought he must have used all his energy to call me from the other room. "James," he said again. "My boy."

"I'm here," I said, feeling a tear in my eye. He had seemed to grow so much weaker in the past few months. Every day he seemed more tired, more vacant, as my parents had done.

"Sit down." He pointed to the chair with his eyes as if his body was almost frozen stiff. His arms were resting on the armrests of the chair and his legs sat pressed together with his feet touching on the floor.

I sat down.

"What's wrong, Bernard?" A tear came down from my eye and I brushed it off with my sleeve.

Bernard opened his eyes wide enough to look at me. His face was still and serious. He looked so worried as if a shield of strength he'd been holding all around him had just fallen apart and I could finally see the real, vulnerable him.

He opened his mouth to talk, but no sound came out, so he weakly cleared his throat and then began in a soft, husky voice, "I'm sorry to tell you. You're not going to like this."

"What is it, Bernard?" I said through falling tears. He looked so saddened by my obvious worry. I knew it wasn't going to be good news, and he knew I knew that, which made him even more worried and I could hear the shaking in his voice. After a few moments of silence, he replied,

"I'm dying, James." He looked at me as if to ask me to respond, as if no more needed to be said on his part, his eyebrows rising, sadly. His eyes looked old, weak and pitiful.

I said nothing.

Then he continued. "I've got cancer. There is nothing the doctors can do. I have been to so many appointments over the last year; but no, there is nothing they can do for me. They have told me it's terminal."

Bernard seemed to put on a stronger and stronger face as he spoke, as if he felt he had to be strong for me.

"I was so worried about the future of Belet. I didn't want it to fall into ruins after three hundred years of my family's hard work. I was so worried, James. I prayed to God for an answer." He stopped talking and swallowed. It sounded difficult and painful. Then he breathed out heavily. "Then one morning, I find you asleep outside my shed. At first I thought it was a sign; that it was meant to be." His voice became weaker and weaker until it became hardly more than a whisper. "I didn't want you to take on the vineyard because you felt obliged to, so I didn't want you to know about my illness. As I got to know you I wanted you to make up your own mind, based on your own life, your own dreams. Finally it felt as though the time was

101

right to tell you. You've made up your own mind and I'm so thankful that it is as I hoped and prayed it would be."

"Bernard," I whimpered, weakly. "Of course I will look after the vineyard." I smiled, through my wet face. "I need the vineyard as much as it needs me."

I think I saw Bernard smile ever so slightly but it was difficult to tell as his face was so still and seemed so much more withered than even the last time I had seen him.

"Bernard," I said, "how, how long do they say, you've, you've…"

"Not long, James," Bernard replied, sounding somehow more peaceful than before. "Not long."

I knew how much the vineyard meant to Bernard. It had been his life's work. I knew he would die happy if he knew I was taking over. He trusted me. I'm pretty sure he loved me.

"I've got to a ripe old age," he continued.

"Are you sure I am the right person to take over?" I asked Bernard, knowing the answer, but asking out of duty.

"James, my boy," Bernard said, sounding suddenly more alive than a minute ago. "You are the one, the only one."

I smiled and said, "Okay."

Then, Bernard paused and looked like he was thinking deeply about something. "Unless you find an Abraham or a Belet."

At first I thought he was joking, but then I realised he wasn't smiling.

"You see," he continued, "in my father's will he wrote that Belet should always stay in the family," he said this hesitantly, as if he thought he was betraying me. "I have only known you three months, James. But to me, you are family. That is why I am happy, more than happy, for you to take over when I'm gone."

"Of course," I replied, knowing how torn Bernard must have been feeling between his feelings and his tradition and respect for his deceased father.

"But anyway," he said again, with a slight smile re-appearing on his face, "we don't need to think about that." He paused. "There aren't any."

I smiled, but only ever so slightly. It didn't feel right. Then, we sat in silence for a few minutes as his smile turned back into a withered natural frown and he slowly drifted off to sleep.

I continued to sit there, listening to his heavy breathing for another five minutes, taking in everything he had just told me. I was to be the saviour of Belet; I'd be making Bernard as proud as I'm sure my parents would now be.

I loved Bernard and I dreaded him being gone, however in knowing that I was letting him die happy, part of me pondered on the idea of being completely alone on the vineyard and I almost, guiltily admittedly, smiled at the idea of it. I'd be truly alone, truly at peace. No one could touch me. The noise of the busy rush hour trains and the filling high school playground would be such distant memories I wouldn't even be able to imagine them, and I'd instead be truly at one with the land, with the field, with the open, everlasting solitude. I would belong.

I quietly left the living room so to not wake Bernard and trying to stay as silent as possible, I walked up the stairs, back up the corridor and up to my bedroom, noticing that the rain in the darkness outside the window subsided and the outside light had come on, revealing that the water blurring the window had trickled down to the ground just enough for me to see through the glass again.

Ten

Over the course of the next week and a half, I continued to work on the fields but most of my time was spent talking to people over the phone, arranging visits to the vineyard and logistics. There seemed to always be something to do. However, I was pleased that my mind was being kept occupied so that I didn't have time to think about Bernard who was getting weaker and weaker with every passing day.

He had now stopped working on the land and instead just spent his time pottering around the house doing odd jobs and trying to keep busy. Once or twice a day he would go for a short walk around the patio to get some fresh air and sun and almost every time, I would see him pause and look out onto the vineyard as if it was the gravestone of an old friend.

Bernard had told me that he had written his will and he was leaving the house and all of its land to me. I would own it and be free to do what I liked with it. Of course, I planned on continuing to run it as a vineyard and I promised him that I would look after it when the time came.

It was coming up to the middle of August and the harvest was drawing near. I knew how much it meant to Bernard. It would almost certainly be his last. I could feel his pain as I watched him from a distance staring into the vineyard. He never cried in front of me; I don't think he liked to appear weak, but I could have sworn I could see a tear glistening on his cheek in the sun.

****

I had spent most of the day walking people through the vineyard and discussing figures with them with regard to them investing in our wine through something called 'en premier,' which means buying the wine at a discounted price before it is bottled, to then sell on when it is. I used to deal with similar things when I worked in banking. By the end of the day, I was tired out from all the number crunching and was looking forward to some peace and quiet.

The investors had been gone for about half an hour and I was still sitting in the same room we had been having the meeting in, appreciating the silence. The sun was starting to set outside and the light seemed to have a strange and eerie feeling to it. I just sat there, looking out at it.

I must have almost drifted off to sleep, even though I'm sure my eyes were still open, when Bernard called me from the doorway.

I had been helping him up the stairs for the past few days as he had become too weak to walk up them on his own.

I got up straight away and after pausing for a moment to get my own balance, walked towards him at the door and he turned to let me take his arm. It took a good five minutes to help him up the two flights of stairs to his bedroom and onto his bed and when he finally lay back he looked exhausted and empty, as if he was drained almost completely of life.

His bed was large and grand with four mahogany posts on each corner. He had a bookshelf and a desk and a small wooden chair in the corner, a large wardrobe and a big arched window with a crossed diagonal stripe. Outside the window, in the day, you could have a good view of the vineyard, the lines of grape bushes spread out like a huge vast maze. But at night time, you couldn't see anything out of the window, only darkness.

By the time I was in Bernard's bedroom, the sun had almost completely set and I could just see a faint line between the land and the sky and the outline of the shed about two hundred feet away. I heard Bernard struggling to get beneath his sheets so I turned away from the window and helped him in.

He was like a dead weight, but I managed. He lay there for a bit, half asleep, me sitting on the edge of the bed, making sure he fell asleep all right, before I left the room. He started to breathe a bit deeper so I thought he had drifted off but then I heard him say something in a voice so croaky and weak it was just about audible:

"Thank you, son."

I looked at him and his eyes were closed. I leant across the bed and kissed him on the forehead. He didn't smile; he just continued to breathe deeply. I put my hand on his head and stroked his hair back just once, before getting up off his bed and walking to the door.

I turned back and looked at him and smiled to myself. I hadn't felt such a bond with anyone since my parents were alive. I had grown to love him as a father. I switched the light off and quietly left the room.

Bernard didn't wake up.

****

I had Bernard buried in a cemetery called Chartreuse in Bordeaux. As I arranged the funeral, I realised just how alone Bernard was, and how alone he must have been before I arrived at his vineyard. There was nobody for me to contact to tell about his death and of course, there was nobody but me at his funeral. It was utterly astounding how such a charismatic and joyous man such as Bernard could somehow go by unnoticed by society. It felt like he had just slipped away without the world knowing. I wondered what would have happened if I had never met him. Would he still be lying on his bed, cold and stiff? How long would it have been before he was discovered?

At Eric's funeral, earlier that year, I had felt like a bit of an intruder. I had walked off into the woods to let his family and close friends be alone with their grief. Standing next to Bernard's grave, I couldn't have felt more different. I was the one, the only one. Looking back, it was strange to think how, if it hadn't been for Eric's suicide, I would have never ended up standing by Bernard's grave. He still would have died and his body and the vineyard would now have been left to rot. I felt such grief, but such meaning as I stood in that cemetery, dried tears on my face, looking down at Bernard's gravestone through slightly blurry eyes.

****

I arrived back at Belet in the evening, just as the sun was beginning to set and as I walked through the gates, it had a certain eeriness to it. The pathway that lead past the shed and up to the mansion seemed so cold and as I walked, I looked out onto the vineyard, which itself seemed so vast and still; I walked as fast as I could without running towards the big black door of the mansion. I didn't feel

107

safe. Everything felt too silent, too calm, as if I was in the eye of a storm. But I knew, as I scrabbled in my pocket for the key, that there was no storm, other than the one that had been raging in my head my whole life.

I locked the door behind me and immediately turned every light on I could see. The house was always quite dark, even in the day time because of the lack of windows, but by the time I sat down in the front living room, I could see through the big arched window that the sun had already almost set.

Sitting there, on my own, I couldn't help but feel a sense of loneliness coming over me, a real, overwhelming sense of loneliness. The flickering light from the shed in the distance, shone through the glass and it reminded me of the night time view from my old apartment in St John's Wood. For a few moments, I imagined that I was there, looking down at the houses and the shops and the roads below, car lights whizzing silently past, eight storeys below. I felt surrounded, I felt in the middle of it, I felt safe; a warmth started to grow inside me.

I snapped back into reality, got up and walked out the room. It had only been a thought, just a small, meaningless thought, but even just that worried me, almost disturbed me. I walked into the library.

Most of the books were in French and the majority of the ones that were in English, I had already read back in school. There were a few that I hadn't read, but they were long and I wasn't in the right mind-set to start, so I just sat there.

I thought about Bernard and felt both a deep sadness and a wonderful happiness at the same time; I thought about the harvest and felt a terrible anxiety waiting to come out when the time drew nearer. I thought about the promise

I had made to Bernard, that I would look after the vineyard and make sure it doesn't go into ruin. Then, as I looked around at the books piled all over the wooden shelves and tables, I began to think about school and then, uncontrollably and eventually acceptingly, I started to think about London.

****

The harvest was due to start in just a couple of weeks and there was still so much to organise. I needed to contact all the contract workers that would arrive a few days before the harvest to get ready for the next months' work, whilst also arranging all the tours and the meetings and continuing to look after the land. I had a lot to do and I was somewhat dreading it.

The days rolled by and before I knew it, the harvest was in one weeks' time. I had already arranged for all the contract staff to come and was pretty much prepared for it to begin. The grape bushes were thick and green and almost ready to be picked. All I had to do now was wait for everything to begin.

****

It was seven in the morning and I was woken up by a knocking at the door. It took me a few moments to come round. I had been deep in a dream and woke up so suddenly it felt like I was still in it.

I had had the dream before and it filled me with the same dread as the last time. I was back in the windowless, doorless white room, just lying there, staring at the ceiling, not even needing to look at the walls for I knew in my heart that there was no escape. I had the feeling inside me that I knew a door was about to appear, I think because of the fact I was partly remembering the last time I had dreamt it. I just lay there, waiting, knowing that even when the door did appear on the white wall, it would lead to nowhere and there was no escape.

When I came round and realised that there was somebody waiting at the door, I felt so relieved and calm.

I was already wearing pyjama trousers so I shoved on my top and my slippers and dashed down the two flights of stairs to the door. It had only taken me about a minute, but I wondered how long he had been knocking for before I'd woken up.

I got to the door and started to unlock the two locks. As I did, I had a strange and terrifying thought that it would be Bernard. I opened the door. Of course it wasn't.

Instead, standing at the door, was a man in a checkered tweed suit. He must have been about mid-forties, six foot tall with a rough beard and short but messy brown hair with several streaks of grey.

"Hello," he said, in a voice that sounded like it had never been settled in one place. It was a mix of accents that sounded mainly English, with hints of French, German, Italian – everything.

"Hello," I said. "How can I help you?" 'What is he doing knocking at seven in the morning?' I thought to myself.

He didn't say anything for a second, just looked at me, similar to the way Bernard used to sometimes. It was almost as if he had forgotten his lines. Then he said something.

"Who are you?"

"My name is James," I replied, "and you are?" Then I waited again for him to respond as he looked at me as if he was dreading having to tell me what he was about to tell me.

"My name is John Abraham," he said, with a serious and anxious face. "Where is Bernard? It has taken me so long to finally track him down. Am I right that he lives here?" his anxiety seemed to grow as he spoke.

"Who are you to him?" I asked, hoping he wouldn't respond in the way I was painfully certain he would.

"I'm his son," he said, giving a weak and forced smile as if he too was dreading *me* responding in a way in which *he* was painfully certain I would.

"Come in," I said, stepping back from the door, and he did.

Eleven

I have never known the sunrise anywhere in the world to be quite like the sunrise over Belet. It was so much more than just beautiful. It was calming, it was forgiving, it was forgetting.

Quite often, I would get up while it was still dark and go and sit on the rocking chair by the shed. I would edge my way through the dark, slowly, being careful not to trip over. The view of the vineyard was just as good from the patio of the mansion, but there was something about sitting by the shed that felt special. I felt more a part of the land than I did when I sat next to the mansion. I felt like I really belonged; sitting on the wooden beams at one with nature. Maybe it was because it reminded me of the night I arrived at Belet, the peace I felt, the confidence that I had made the right decision.

I would sit in the dark in my dressing gown and feel the early morning chill on my face, listening to the sounds of birds, somehow lighting up the darkness with their high pitched chirps.

Every sunrise would remind me of the fact that I now belonged. I'd wait for it to rise on the horizon and know in my heart that when it did, I would still be sitting here, and I would look out to the grape bush lined fields that stretched into the distance and be content.

I didn't want to run away anymore.

John didn't cry when I told him that his father had died. He just had an empty and accepting look in his eyes as if he was far too used to misery. It was almost as if he felt as though he had no right to grieve.

John told me that his mother's name was Julia Abraham. She brought him up on her own in London in a small one-bedroom apartment. She worked in two jobs to pay all the bills and to pay for John's care. He had severe bipolar and needed to have psychotherapy sessions once a week every week.

When John was ten, his mental condition took a turn for the worse when he ran away from home and jumped off a bridge. He insisted it wasn't a suicide attempt but just an impulsive act without thought about the consequences. It sounded as though he wasn't in control of his actions.

Julia finally accepted after years of trying that she couldn't give John the medical and psychological attention he needed and she did what she had always been desperate not to have to do; she put her son in a home.

Several more years went by and she visited him as much as she was allowed to, but as John aged into a teenager, he realised how much of a burden he had been on his mother, but he knew he could never change. He had a condition and he had to accept it. But he didn't have to accept continuing to be a burden. So, one day, when he was fourteen, he packed his rucksack with all his most important belongings, wrote a suicide note and ran away. John had no intention of killing himself, but he knew it would be far easier for his mother if, at least in her mind, there was closure.

The rest he told me, in his life anyway, was a blur of merging chapters, his life a concoction of drugs, alcohol and desperate crime.

John told me that quite a few years ago, he had learned that his mother had returned to her old home in France and had settled down. He knew he would never be able to see her again after all, she thought he was dead.

Nonetheless, John kept tabs on her and he tried to remain as close as possible to her without her knowing he was there. Sometimes he told me, he regretted making the choice he made, but he knew in his heart that it was the right thing to do. He watched from a distance as his mother settled down with Bernard, then unaware that he was his father.

When Julia gave birth to her second son, John knew it was time to stop watching and move on. He just couldn't bear the unintentional betrayal.

After many years of living in various countries and multiple attempts at starting afresh, John finally accepted that he couldn't continue living his life in the shadow of his troubled past, so he flew to Belet in the hope of finding his mum.

He soon found out that she had been gone for years.

John told me he was tired of running, tired of searching, tired of everything, so he stopped and stayed in France. He took a job in a department store and rented an apartment in town.

Then one day John received a letter in the post. He showed it to me. It was in English and it read:

'Dear John,

This letter may come as a surprise to you and what you are about to read may shock you, so please take a moment and pull up a chair.

114

You do not know me but I know you. I know you very well. I have been keeping an eye on you since you were a boy.

My name is Manrico Marcellus and I am head of the French Wine Association. After much discussion, the council and I have decided that writing to you is the right thing to do.

Let me begin.

Forty-five years ago, I had a conversation with a somewhat distressed pregnant lady named Julia Abraham. She was on her way to London to start a new life. She made me promise her personally that I would never contact her unborn child in years to come; precisely what I am doing now. She was desperate for you to never find out where you came from and you were yet to have even been born.

I think she saw what the vineyard lifestyle does to a man in her husband. If you are not careful, if you don't take measures, it can isolate you from the world. It is very easy to fall out of sync with society and become a recluse.

Your father's name is Bernard Abraham and he is the owner of Chateau Belet in Bordeaux. Your mother left him following several years of marital unrest and moved to London where you were born and raised.

Following your 'suicide', your mother returned to Belet desperate to be in a place she felt she had support to keep on going. We all thought you were dead until I, several years after your mother's death, which I know you know about, rather disturbingly discovered that you were living right here in France.

Your father is very sick, John. I am sorry I haven't written until now but it is that which made me come to the decision after all these years.

Now of course, even though you know nothing about wine, the council have been urging and urging me to write to you to tell you to go to Belet and at least play a part in the running of the vineyard. The wine business is a game of tradition and the value of Belet will fall rapidly if the Abraham name falls from above its doors.

But do not think John for a second that that is the main reason for my writing. I have kept my promise to Julia for long enough and you have been kept in the dark about who you really are for far too long.

I know sorry is not enough but I hope you at least understand why I couldn't write to you sooner.

The reason I have kept tabs on you since you were a child is because I secretly always knew this day would come and even despite promising myself that I would never break the promise I had made to your mother, even though in my heart I knew she was right about what was best for you, I knew deep down that one day I would be writing this letter, and I didn't just want to put it in a bottle and chuck it into the sea hoping it would find you. I needed to know where you would be.

Please know that Bernard never knew you existed and he still doesn't. So if you do decide to pay him a visit, break the news lightly to him. As I mentioned, he is extremely unwell.

Just to remind you, it's Chateau Belet in Bordeaux.

Warmest regards,

Manrico.'

John told me that he spent a few days struggling to believe what he had just heard then a few days comprehending it and then a few more days plucking up the courage to come to Belet. One week after he received the letter, he arrived at my door.

****

As I lay in bed that night, trying desperately to get to sleep, John's story played over and over in my head. As I wriggled under my duvet, my thoughts turned to Bernard and the promise I had made to him. I had sworn that I would look after the place he had dedicated his life to.

I came to Belet to escape my responsibilities and to live in a place where it could be just me and the land, not to run a vineyard on my own. As much as I wanted to keep my promise and maintain his life's work, an ever-growing part of me felt as though I was losing my way.

I had had this idea of belonging. I saw it as a place one could reach and stay because one wanted to, not because one had to, where one could look out into the distant fields and see that the grass was greener where they stood, but as I lay in bed that night, I started to think that maybe obligation was all belonging could ever be.

Bernard had told me that I was second only to an Abraham. He had dreaded having the vineyard fall into someone else's name just as much as I dreaded having to run the place. It was then that I started to think about how maybe John turning up at the door had been an answer to both our prayers.

I pondered on the idea for a few moments before the sight of the grape bushes glistening all around me in the sun spread through my mind and I fell into a peaceful sleep almost immediately, unable to differentiate my sleepy thoughts from the beautifully calm dream I was falling silently into.

****

I woke up the next morning certain of the decision I must have made subconsciously the night before.

John was already sitting in the lounge when I came downstairs in my dressing gown at seven o'clock.

He was facing out of the window, but it seemed as though he wasn't watching the world outside. It was as if the glass pane was more of a mirror for him to look back at his own demons. He didn't hear me at the door, so I stood still for a second and looked across the room at him, half empathising with his hidden grief, but half revelling in the fact that for the first time since I arrived at Belet, it was I that felt at home.

John turned around as if he had suddenly realised my presence. He jumped up when he caught my eye.

"Sleep well?" I said with a welcoming smile.

John crinkled his mouth. "I've had better nights." It looked like he thought he'd better say something. "Beautiful view of the vineyard." He gestured with his eyes to the window he had been vacantly staring into.

A smile spread across my face, "It is," I said. "Come on," I beckoned with a warm authority, "let's get some croissants. There's something I want to talk to you about."

I couldn't help but hear Bernard in me, as John walked quietly but swiftly over, similar to how a child would do who had finally found their way back home.

****

As I walked down the pathways between the grape bushes that afternoon, I couldn't help but feel a bit of guilt that I had gone back on my word to Bernard. However when I really thought about it, I was almost certain that his desire to have the vineyard continue in his name would

118

have overridden his desire to have me take over. John was his son and it wasn't his fault he had never had the opportunity to have a relationship with his father. The way I saw it, handing the vineyard over to John was the least I could do to make up for the lifetime of misfortune that had been handed to him.

John was excited about the prospect of finally being able to settle down and call a place his own. I think he would have been happy to be given the chance to settle down anywhere, but the fact that it was his family home made it all the more special.

The only problem was John had never worked on a vineyard in his life and he was in dire need of training before he took over. But who was I to say that somebody wasn't capable of learning a completely new field in a short space of time. He certainly wasn't short of work experience, albeit, completely different sectors, but I had faith that his determination alone would be enough to get him to the standard he needed to be to successfully run Belet.

I had promised to run the harvest and make sure everything ticked over the way Bernard told me it had to. I would finish dealing with the investors and the buyers and all the companies and then soon after, I would sign the legal documents overriding Bernard's will to put the vineyard and the Château in his son's name. Then, at last, I could finally get back to the life I had come here for.

"James!" I heard John's voice and turned to see him walking hurriedly over. The grape bushes were thick and leafy and stood about six feet high so you could only see somebody on the vineyard if they walked onto your pathway.

I hadn't seen John since the morning. I had advised, as Bernard had advised me, that he should go and familiarise himself with the land. After all, the best way of learning where you are is by getting lost.

The vineyard was a bit like a huge maze, however it was ultimately secluded from the surrounding land so it was impossible to get completely lost as if you stayed on the pathways; you would always eventually find your way back. A low fence surrounded the grape fields, but due to the slope of the land, you were unable to see the fence from the vast majority of places and at this time of year, when the vines were high, you were unable to see it from anywhere.

The only way out that wouldn't walk you into the fence were the woods, where the pathways between the grape bushes faded gradually into the dark, dry brambles that became the woodland.

"Have you familiarised yourself yet, John?" I asked as he slowed towards me.

"Thought I'd never find you," he replied as if he hadn't heard me.

"Whereabouts have you been?"

"I thought I'd stick to one path and walk straight. I figured that would be the best way of learning the size of the place." I was waiting for the 'but'.

Then I got in first. "It doesn't quite work, does it?"

John smiled. "Not at all, James, not at all."

I knew as well as anyone that it was almost impossible to plan a route through the vineyard without the use of a map, unless you knew it well. Even though every path was dead straight, there were just far too many crossing in and out of each other at every angle imaginable to keep track of where you had already walked.

"I'm just finishing checking these bushes down here, then we can head back," I said, turning my attention back to the grape bushes.

"Okay," John replied. "Whenever you're ready."

I started to brush through the vines with my hands to check the quality of the grapes in this section, to see how close they were to being ready for the harvest. Then I heard John say something that completely stopped me in my tracks.

"I managed to find the woods." He looked at me as if for me to congratulate him on his navigational skills, but instead I gave him an unintended stern look as if he had said something that had offended me. I then smiled to hide my concern and said, "Glad to hear it," as I drew my eyes back to the grapes, my mind still fixed entirely on what he had just said.

I had thought about the woods many times in the last four months, but for some reason someone else mentioning them made me almost shudder. A few hours after I had told Bernard I'd been to the woods and seen how distressed he had become, I'd assured him that I wouldn't return to them and he didn't tell me otherwise. Since he had passed away I felt even more obliged to keep my word, but hearing them mentioned reminded me how desperate I was to find out what secret Bernard had been hiding, even at the cost of dishonouring him.

'You didn't turn left?' I remembered him saying all those months ago in a voice so consumed with buried terror; you could almost hear his words trembling.

As I counted the grapes, almost forgetting John's waiting presence just ten feet away from me, I unwittingly accepted that I'd have to return.

Twelve

Tiny raindrops tapped gently on the wooden roof of the shed. From the rocking chair, I could see the decking turning gradually darker as the light rain fell. I was sheltered as the top of the shed hung in a chalet style over where I sat, but I could feel the dampness in the air.

I looked out at the thick grape bushes, stretching into the distance, looking wild and fresh. The atmosphere was dark and grey, but the lamp above me and the slight humidity in the early morning air gave everything a warm feeling.

I could just about make out what time it was on my watch in the dark; it was ten to six. As I rolled my wrist round to make certain of the faint hands on my watch, I noticed how rough and worn my skin was; how natural I felt.

It was about five o'clock when I crawled out of bed, feeling relaxed to a state that felt hardly any different from tiredness, but refreshed from a comfortable nights' sleep. I had changed out of my pyjamas into slightly more hardwearing loungewear as I noticed grey clouds stirring outside my bedroom window. I'd walked downstairs in my socks and put on my waterproof slippers that were waiting for me at the front door before walking out to head for the rocking chair.

I had been sitting there for about half an hour in the warm drizzling rain, when the golden rays started to rise up behind the distant grapevines.

As I watched the bright yellow light spread over the green of the fields and through every path between the grape bushes, I could have sworn that I could almost feel some of its warming rays seeping into me.

****

With the arrival of about twenty-five workers throughout the course of the morning, the harvest had begun.

Harvest time in Bordeaux is the busiest time of the year. Mostly, throughout the course of the year, nothing really happens on the vineyards. The land is empty, other than the growing vines. But when harvest comes, and it's usually around late summer for the majority of wines, the vineyards change suddenly from quiet, tranquil escapes to busy, bustling places.

Wine is big business. I know from the other side what a huge market it is, but it's strange to see how something as number driven and modern as the investment market in the western world, all leads back to the vineyards; places that haven't changed throughout the generations, both in vines and in ownership.

Well, apart from Château Belet.

Every harvest, which is once a year, has what is called its own vintage. That is just a fancy way of saying its year. It is a way for consumers of wine, or should I say, investors of wine, with the idea of consumers of wine in their minds, to calculate how much a certain bottle is going to rise in value.

This would be the vintage of 2016. It would mark the passing of Bernard and therefore for reasons of respect, amongst other things, the chances are the wine would be popular.

Investors, I'm sure, will do their research and realise that now the well respected and experienced Bernard Abraham has died, leaving no even remotely experienced person in his place, Belet's wine is about to start going downhill. Whether or not this will make them want to buy this year's vintage, Bernard's last vintage, with the hope that it will be worth a fortune in years to come when it is the only remaining high quality wine from Belet, or whether they believe that it won't rise in value because Belet's reputation is going to fall so dramatically it will override the quality of this year's, I do not know. All I do know, is it is going to be an interesting vintage.

But, if I am honest, I care little about the vintage or the money or even the wine. All I care about is Belet's reputation, and the only reason I care about that is because of the promise I had made to its owner.

Wine is the sort of product with no monopolies whatsoever in the market. People who drink wine always look around for new products; it is part of the experience of buying it – trying new. Yes, some are more popular than others, but the majority of vineyards never will have to worry about running out of business and that is why I do not have to worry about my future at Belet.

I will make all the money I need and the bottles will keep on going out to the world, sharing our grapes with people as far afield as Asia and Australia.

The whole wine business seems to work automatically and even though the people are at its heart, they seem to just be another piece in the natural wine making puzzle, no different from the vines or the grapes.

I have to admit, it somewhat sickened me to be thinking about business and investing when the weather today was so delightful.

The sun shone down so strong, it drenched the thick green grape bushes, the dark red grapes glistening beautifully in the light. Everything – the grape bushes, the grass of the paths, the grapes themselves even – appeared so dry and still, so consumed by the light and the heat of the afternoon sun.

Looking around as I walked through the pathways close to the mansion, I could see all the grape pickers that had arrived earlier in the day. They all wore shorts, linen shirts and sunhats, the ladies wore the same; it was clear that this was a place for work, not fashion, and that made it a beautiful scene.

Then I saw someone I recognised.

"John!" I called out and raised my hand so he would notice me. He didn't. He was busy picking grapes just along the path with a couple of workers. It was highly satisfying to watch as he taught them a few tricks I had taught him earlier that week, so I did watch for a minute before I called again from close by.

He looked up.

"James!" he said, "Been hiding have you?"

"Always," I replied, with a smile.

Then John smiled and I shook his hand.

"Good work," I said, with a slightly more serious look on my face. "Good work."

He let out a noise rather difficult to explain. It was a half-light laugh, half sigh of relief. It sounded half like he was happy with what I just said and half like he was deep in thought about how he had finally found a place he belonged. There was so much meaning in that noise.

"Now back to it," I said, putting on a strict voice, but in a comical, light-hearted way, and I continued down the grassy path before I could see him smile again or make any more deeply heartfelt noises.

As I walked, I noticed how the path behind me, the path that lead through the grape bushes that the workers had been working on, seemed to be growing ever wider, ever more sparse, with every grape they picked.

****

Our wine wasn't bottled on site. Most vineyards produce the wine from start to finish; they grow the grapes, pick them, press them and bottle the wine in the bottling house. Belet had no bottling house. I had asked Bernard why and he had told me that it is just the way it was.

We were not short of money. Bernard's will granted me full access to the company's bank account and I knew we were very, very comfortable. It would be a large investment to install all the machines necessary and a building to house them in at Belet, but I would have thought it would be worth it. Obviously Bernard did not as he made sure his will didn't grant me authority to erect such a thing after his passing.

It occurred to me that Bernard had seen Belet as more of a home, more of a place to adhere to tradition and more of an escape from the big, intimidating world, than a business.

Every time he would go out to have meetings at the bank or official lunches in Paris, he would come home in a panic. I would watch from outside the shed as he would frantically unlock the gate at the entrance and almost run up the path to the door of the mansion. It looked as though he thought he was being chased. Why he felt like that I did not know. I told myself it was because all he had ever known was life on the vineyard, but I had a feeling inside me that his fear of the outside world was down to something else; that he was running up the path away from something more than just the idea of the busy world.

But after all, who was I to judge? The day I walked through those open gates for the first time, I was running like I had never run before, and even though in reality I was crawling slowly so not to trip in the pitch black darkness, in my mind I was sprinting as fast as my legs would carry me, away from the life I had just escaped from.

It was rather frustrating, however, having to send van after van back and forth from Belet to the bottling site. Even though it was only a mile or so down the road, the fact I had to walk for fifteen minutes every time I needed to check something, felt like an effort for nothing but my frustration always quickly turned to guilt when I thought about how all Bernard had wanted, was to maintain his family's tradition. He had been unable to do it the way he had always wanted by having a son, at least as far as he knew anyway, so I had no right to be annoyed about something as minor as an offsite bottling house.

Although I did wonder how Bernard had always managed without a car. I planned to buy one as even though I knew I would only really use it at harvest time as the rest of the year I had little intention of leaving the vineyard, I felt that after all the work I was putting into making this year's harvest a success, I had earned myself a present.

I stood and watched two men lift a huge crate of plump red grapes off the ground and into the back of a van. It looked heavy; I was glad I didn't have to lift it. The heat beaming down was strong. I could see a glimmering everywhere I looked and I knew that the sandy path under my feet was dry and hot. I wiped the sweat off my forehead and brushed my dark hair back away from my eyes, which felt like a soft radiator as I ran my fingers through it in a slow, smooth motion.

After putting the crate down, one of the men grabbed hold of one of the sides and shook vigorously. The red grapes at the top of the heap inside the crate bounced around whilst the grapes underneath remained still as if the sheer volume of them had formed a solid object inside the crate. The man that had just shaken it gave the other man a look of approval as if to say, 'this crate isn't going anywhere' and then they both walked off, nodding their heads at me as they passed, back down the path and into the bustling vineyard.

I stood still and looked up to the blue sky, having to close my eyes from the brightness, consciously appreciating the sun's warming glow on my face in the middle of a long and draining day. My head was full of all the tasks I needed to remember, all the jobs waiting for me, the jobs that only I could do. No one else could sign the contracts with the buyers and no one else could pay in our cheques. This was *my* operation and it was *my* name on the bottles.

I reluctantly looked back down and opened my eyes. The white van was right in front of me, its shadow, short and dark, lay beside it on the flat sand. I walked round to the front passenger door, opened it, put my foot on the step, feeling the sweat on my shins rubbing against my light trousers, and I climbed in.

The driver immediately put his foot on the gas and after a few seconds of what sounded like a choking machine, the van pulled slowly away. I looked out of the window and saw the sand blowing up into the air. It looked as hot as the fake leather seat I was trying to get comfortable in. As the van sped up along the dirt track towards the gates and the sun beamed down through the windscreen, surrounding me so much so that squinting hardly helped, I accepted that trying to get comfortable was a futile task.

I had 'grinned and beared' the heat and the light and the bumpy road, which threw me around the front of the van like a rag doll, even with the broken seatbelt on, for five long minutes, when the driver finally pulled in to the driveway of the bottling house and not a second too soon.

A thick line of high trees separated the premises from the road and brought me some long awaited shade from the relentless sun. I looked out of the windscreen that seemed to have a layer of dust covering it, at the building. It was a simple design, rectangular and solid looking, dark grey stone with a concrete chimney on either side. The strange part was, similarly to the mansion at Belet, it had very few windows. The building looked about three to four storeys tall and it was about three times as wide as it was tall, but it was difficult to tell how tall it was as there was nothing obviously separating the floors. It was dark, daunting and imposing and as the van slowly drove towards the front door which I soon realised was about three times the size of a normal door and I realised how big the place was, I couldn't help but feel somewhat intimidated.

A small group of men were already waiting on the dirt drive when the van pulled up and we climbed out. The driver unlocked the back door and the men got to work on carrying the crates inside. I stood for a second and watched and then once the large crate I had seen ten minutes earlier had been picked up, I followed the men to the door of the dreaded building.

As one of the men pushed open the front door which wasn't locked, with what looked like most of his strength, I envisioned seeing a huge hallway with a staircase leading up, red drapes hanging down and curtains blowing like ghosts over spider web covered stained glass windows, but in reality, all I saw was a small corridor with a door on the right that said, 'sorting room', and a door on the left that said 'bottling room'. The last man pushed the front door shut behind him.

I waited in that corridor while everybody including the driver walked down the corridor to the end and through a door I couldn't see at first, with a sign that had been worn off. They all walked through and the door swung shut behind them. For about five seconds I stood in silence, slightly puzzled as to what it was I should be doing with myself. It seemed to me like everybody knew what they were doing, and I'm sure they did. After being in control since Bernard's passing, I had grown use to the feeling and I had to sometimes remind myself that at the end of the day, in the wine business; I was the new one.

I found myself staring at the sign on the door on the right, 'Bottling Room'. I suddenly realised that it was handwritten, but it was so neat it looked like it had been typed. Everything here seemed to be so old, so simple but so well structured and precise. I turned the knob on the door and it felt like it was broken which surprised me, having thought what I had just thought. I pushed the door but it didn't budge. After a while spent turning the knob back and forth and wriggling it around, it finally clicked and I felt the door come ajar.

I walked through.

In the middle there was a large iron machine with a conveyer belt wrapping itself around it. There wasn't much else in the room; it was big and spacious and looked as though there had long ago been more machines that had been got rid of. On the conveyer belt there stood three bottles, each full of red wine and corked.

The second I spotted them I walked straight over and picked one up.

There was the label Bernard had shown me several months back, wrapped neatly around the dark red bottle. It was old-fashioned looking, almost purposely ancient; a small picture of a painting of our Château, and a crest of leaves and grapes wrapping around the name that took centre stage; 'Bernard James'.

I felt goose pimples on my back and a feeling inside me, a feeling of success – *satisfaction and success*. I held the bottle to my chest and closed my eyes tightly. I thanked Bernard that he had given me the opportunity to find my place; I thanked god that I had had the courage to do what I knew was right all those months ago.

The bottle was so much more than just a symbol for the success of Belet, it was a symbol for the success of my journey; the journey of my heart. It was a symbol of belonging. It was here because of me and I was here because of it and we were both right there, right then, standing together in the bottling room, right where we belonged.

Before long I opened my eyes. I knew I was too busy to get carried away with my emotion. Part of me felt an even greater sense of success because of the fact I had reached a place where I was happy to be too busy to have time to care about such things as my mental state.

My eyes opened and I was looking automatically right at the surface of the dark red wine lying flat on the inside of the slightly lighter toned bottle. I stared at it as I moved the bottle in my hand, stared at it as the line of the surface moved in perfect unison with my hand's movement of the bottle, always in line with gravity, always symmetrical with the grey concrete floor of the bottling room.

The feeling of perfection overwhelmed me; the precise symmetry, the invisible lines that could be drawn throughout the wine's surface and the floor and the bottle and my hand. My hand was so still so the wine was just the same. As I stared into it, persuading myself subconsciously that if I looked deep enough I would find something, I began to scare myself into believing that I would, that I would see or realise something that I didn't want to.

Then in a skin tingling moment, I did.

It was the glass of the bottle that held the wine in so perfectly. Even though the wine appeared calm and smooth, it was completely surrounded by the dark red glass. There was a whole sea of apparent freedom held blindly inside a wrapping of glass; trapped, so very trapped because it was completely blind to its entrapment.

I felt my heart beating fast, pumping deeply through the bone and skin of my chest. I felt my breathing deepen and all of a sudden my vision went all blurry as if a mist was filling the room, as if I could no longer see where I was going in time.

I felt the bottle slip through my fingers.

It smashed on the concrete floor.

The noise made me jump, but seemed to pull me out of the anxiety attack I could feel was about to come over me.

My heartbeat began to slow down and my breathing began to soften. As the blur began to die down in my eyes, I saw what lay at my feet; a pile of shattered glass, one large piece, jagged and razor sharp on every edge with a part of the label on, the part that said my name, lying still in the middle of a growing puddle of red liquid, so dark and so rich it looked almost black, like oil or blood.

Thirteen

There was a sense of hostility as I walked through the thin grapevines, stripped of their grapes and leaves. The land felt sparser, more baron, the fields were more open to the landscape around them as if the hidden barricade between the world and I had been stripped of its protective leafy layer.

However, I could still feel the sunlight pouring down onto the dry ground and I squinted as its light sprinkled over the low brown bushes that stretched out into every horizon, painting a skeletal covering onto the rolling hills.

One foot in front of the other, I walked at a constant pace, but without hurrying along the pathways I now knew so well, towards the place I didn't know at all.

It had been a week since the last grape had been plucked and the vineyard was back in silence. After the last few coaches drove away and I was left alone on the sandy path, John busying himself inside the château with his new responsibilities, I looked out onto the vineyard and it resembled a battlefield after the battle had happened. The land was lifeless and had been left behind.

My mind was a concoction of excitement and dread, guilt and gratitude. So many thoughts and feelings running through my head gave me a strange feeling of calm. I think there was just too much going on in my mind to focus on one thing, so I just let all my worries slip out of my body and breathed sighs of relief and peace as I watched them floating away with the breeze.

I just walked, my mind void of feeling, void of constant contemplation, my heart void of the ongoing ache I had grown so used to.

Because even in Belet, even as I sat on the rocking chair and watched the sun rise or strolled along the pathways that stretched over the hills and into the forgiving mist of the horizon, even as I lay down on my own, my back on the warm grass, my eyes to the everlasting sky, greenery surrounding me protectively on every side, still I had something inside me, something deep, deep inside.

I just didn't know what it was, that was causing my heart to inherently ache.

Dried, withered leaves crunched therapeutically under my shoes with every step. I became consciously aware of my connection with the ground and how, since the time I stepped foot on the vineyard about half an hour ago, not a second had gone by where I wasn't at least partially touching the land. One foot touched down on the light brown earth and then the next came up. I was well and truly here and now.

Then I saw the woods appear in the distance.

A shudder came over me. 'What am I going to find?' I thought, my mind persuading me somewhat disappointingly that I would find nothing, but my heart convincing me, excitedly but terrifyingly, that I would.

After about ten minutes of shaky walking, I drew near to the opening. I could feel a sick feeling in my stomach that made me want to lie down, crawl up into a ball and stay as low down as I could, sheltered from the overlooking sky. But I didn't want to stop here. I didn't want to stay.

I thought about turning back as I felt the ground underneath me become leafier and earthier. I thought about how long it would take me if I ran now to get back to a point in the vineyard where I could no longer see the woods, somewhere deep inside the safety of the grape vines where I would know I could no longer see them because they were too far away. I could duck down below the thin bushes and feel the sun and feel safe and protected.

No.

I was here now, right now, right at the place I didn't want to be, and it was time to face what I didn't want to face.

I walked over the leaves and felt the sun go out above me as the overhanging brambles from the trees above and all around me consumed me. For a few minutes I walked, just focusing on my steps and my breathing, trying to stay calm to ensure I didn't turn back. I somewhat left my body for those few minutes, left it in fear, for my mind to be in a safer place.

But when my consciousness came round to where I was, the few minutes of walking without thinking having passed, I suddenly turned round and realised just how deep into the woods I had come and a petrifying chill came over me in the hostile darkness.

The unmaintained dried mud path that I had followed had taken me through the thick woodland and I could see a small opening in the trees about a hundred feet ahead of me.

I walked towards it.

After another ten seconds or so I turned around again and realised I couldn't see the opening, or even any sign of where I had come in. I had only been in the woods a few minutes but already I felt as though I was right in the heart of them.

As I approached the opening, which I could now see was more of a crossroads of various bramble covered paths that stretched throughout, I started to consider if I had really only been in the woods for as little time as I thought I had been. I couldn't see the sky or the sunlight; it felt no different to a cold, dull night time. It felt like no time had passed and it sent a shiver down my spine to contemplate the idea of me having blacked out and in reality, been in here for hours.

What if I had been walking through these woods without realising all day; maybe my sheer fear and terror had been enough to cause my mind to leave my body for far longer than I thought it had. Why couldn't I see the entrance I had only just come through? Why didn't I remember this path from four and a half months ago?

I stopped abruptly and my feet stopped crunching the leaves. The sudden silence scared me. It felt like there was something in it. I looked all around me. The thickness of the woodland was disorientating, if I span around, it would be so easy to get lost, everywhere looked the same; everywhere was dark and dismal and grey. The only reason I felt like I knew roughly where I was, was because I knew, well, I hoped, that I had only been on one path since I had entered through the opening and I could still see the path I was on stretching through the brambles back the way I had come.

The woods felt everlasting, all encompassing, suspiciously even sparser, even more ongoing than the fields and the land outside. Looking back at the peaceful, safe, sunny vineyard filled me with a warming glow deep inside, but the darkness that surrounded me made me think that it was highly possible that the vineyard and the fields were just a small, seemingly open spot inside the woods. Did the woods spread out all around me?

A ghostly, heinous chill suddenly came over me. All the time I had been staying at Belet, all the time I had been tending to the grape bushes, laying peacefully in the sun, sleeping tenderly in my bed, watching the rising sun from the rocking chair in the warm darkness, had I been, all that time, in the heart of the woods?

I physically shook. I was terrified, more terrified than I had ever been before. There was no proof I would even find anything, but I had a feeling deep inside me that I would and that feeling alone was enough to send chills down my spine. Fear itself seemed to grow out of my very being as if I created the terror; I felt as much as the darkness of the woods did.

I looked at my watch, which I could just about make out in the grey, dull atmosphere. My eyes adjusted slowly. Then, my heart honestly skipped a beat.

My watch had stopped.

I looked back again and again to make sure, but then stopped as I felt my body being overwhelmed with shudders and shaking.

How long had I been here?

I felt an ever-growing sense of vulnerability, something I hadn't felt since I was young. I felt like a child, lost in the woods, wanting to be found. I felt I had no power, no strength in my muscles or my mind. I wanted my mum or my dad. I really did. I wanted to be protected, wrapped up, cradled like a baby and carried away in a blanketed basket. I wanted to shrink down to the size I was when I was a new born and whisked away to safety; to the sun.

Then that feeling faded into something else; something far more liberating. Time had stopped. I was here. I was really, really here. Nothing mattered. I was on my own, my parents, society, my sanity, light and now even time had escaped me. All that was standing in-between these trees was me, nothing but me.

Was I home?

I started walking again, steadily, feeling the soil under my shoes.

Then, soon after, I arrived at the crossroads.

The chill came back over me when I looked left.

I stood still for a few moments, remembering all the choices I had made in my life, remembering how I took the road less travelled, the road anyone would have advised me to take and it was taking that very road, that very path in life that had lead me to where I was now. I knew it was time to take that road again.

With just a few glances to the path that lead right and the one that lead straight, both seeming far lighter, far safer, far more open than the dense bramble filled and dark path left, I turned and walked.

I had no intention of backing out now.

Within a minute, everything was darker, everything was thicker. The leaves were larger and thornier. The dried undergrowth was more entangling under my feet. Maybe the path didn't want me down it as much as I didn't want to be down it. But I was down it. I was down it right now, after all these months of dread. Maybe even after a lifetime of unknowing dread. Maybe I was always destined to be right where I was now, even before I came to Belet, even whilst I was content for those brief few years in London.

I was a twelve-year-old boy, hiding in the small opening at the edge of my playground, terrified that I was about to be beaten up, closing my eyes to block out the deafening sound of laughter that I knew was directed at me. I was standing in that opening, not knowing what was the other side of that splintery old fence. What was the other side of that fence? I suddenly thought. Were the woods waiting for me even then? Had they always been waiting for me? Surrounding me? Keeping me locked in?

The undergrowth grew even more entangled with every step, but I carried on trekking through it. I counted the seconds in my head, then the minutes that went by like the passing whistle of the breeze in the browning leaves.

I'd long ago lost count of how long I had been walking down this path, which had quite a while ago become less of a path and more of just a collection of gaps to crawl through between the brambles.

Still, more than ever, something told me to keep going. Something inside me was telling me, with a stronger force than ever, that what I was looking for was coming nearer.

I wasn't even thinking about how I was going to find my way out. I was completely lost. I was at the stage of being lost where one may as well give up on finding a way. I could crawl in any direction and I would have just as much chance of finding my bearings, finding my way out as any other way. I didn't even know how long I had been in the woods for. To be quite honest, I didn't even know if I was still heading left or not. Then, all of a sudden, I realised that I was because with a body and mind overcome with sheer terror, I saw it.

****

I still have that dream quite often; the one where I'm in the room with the white walls. It fills me with the same distressing feeling every time. I'd have thought that in finding a place I belonged, I would have stopped dreaming that I don't belong, that I'm trapped. It's both worrying and rather belittling to realise that sometimes your subconscious mind knows more than your conscious.

I always wake up from that dream in hot sweats. It usually takes me a few moments to come round from it and to realise that I'm not trapped; well, not physically anyway. I will always remain lying down for about a minute, looking around the room, accepting that I'm back in reality and making sure I am not still asleep.

Sometimes, however, just sometimes, even after I wake from the dream and open my eyes wide, even as the light from the morning sunrise shines through my open bedroom window, I still can see the white walls surrounding me.

****

There I was, alone in the woods, the thorny undergrowth wrapping itself around my legs as if I had become part of it, staring in terror at the thing I had come here to find.

There was a small opening that looked as though the years had tangled the outer brambles into it so much so it had become scarcely more than a wild mess, only resembling an opening because of the sheer thickness of the surrounding plantation. In the middle of the opening there stood two large withered stone plates sticking out of the ground. They looked natural, part of the woodland, like they had fallen from the sky or grown out of the ground, but I knew, both from the symmetrical positioning of them in relation to each other and from my gut, that they were not here by nature.

They were gravestones.

Ignoring the sickness that had started to spread throughout my body, I clambered through the shrubbery I had been peering through and onto the slightly lower, for some reason, slightly pricklier undergrowth of the inside of the opening.

I stepped cautiously towards them, as if not wanting to disturb them.

Or, I thought, not wanting to disturb what lay underneath under where I stood.

When I reached them, I crouched down to read their worn engravings, which were just clear enough to make out.

I started with the one on the left;

'Julia Abraham. 10th January 1940 – 12th September 1989.'

I read it, half expecting to see her name. However, the strange, quite chilling part was what was written underneath. Instead of saying, 'Rest in peace,' or 'You will be missed,' all it had engraved on it, in a carving that looked like it had been done by a blunt knife were the words; 'I'm sorry.'

I put my right hand on the undergrowth and edged over to the other gravestone, which stood about one and a half feet to the right;

'Benjamin Abraham. 19th September 1980 – 12th September 1989.'

I looked underneath straight away, just about registering the fact that this boy was only nine years old, desperate to see what this one had engraved on it.

I couldn't help but notice, through eyes blurred with tears of terror, that date, the twelfth of September, scratched onto both gravestones; the same date.

I looked at the carving underneath, which looked like it had been done using the same blunt tool, something slightly sharper than a fingernail and as soon as I saw what it said, all of the chills that had in the past half an hour or so faded away from me came back in a wave of suspicious concern.

I read it through wet eyes, tearing up in terror, as the whistling of the surrounding trees grew louder and louder;

'I'm so sorry,' was the engraving, scratched on so vigorously, I could have sworn I could almost see the long ago faded bloodstains from the fingernails of a man I had spent the last five months living with a man, I suddenly realised, I never knew.

Fourteen

It was October and I had been living in Belet for six months.

I breathed in deeply and could smell the dampness in the air, the fresh moisture in the atmosphere. I hadn't looked at the time this morning, but I could feel it was early.

I have always found that there is such a difference in the morning darkness and the evening darkness. The morning darkness is full of anticipation, full of hope; the evening dark however, is empty and cold.

I have spent so many of my days sitting in the morning dark, waiting for the sunrise and if it is one thing I have found that separates the two darknesses, it is that I swear sometimes I can see the light in the sky even before the sun has come up.

It's that sensation that puts me at peace with the world in the early hours of the morning. That is precisely why my body wakes me up so early most days and it's why I choose almost every time to get out of the comfort of my warm bed and to make the chilly walk to the shed. In my eyes, the sense of peace and belonging I get from that invisible light in the dark sky has always been worth it.

That morning there was not only a constant drizzle, but also a crisp chill in the air. I felt the cold through the thick wool of my dressing gown that was cosy and tight but slightly damp on the outside.

The grape bushes were about three feet high and from the rocking chair, they appeared skeletal and thin, stretching painfully weekly throughout the darkness of the landscape. I could feel the cold wind in the air blowing through their light green leaves. I could feel what the grapevines felt, what the pathways felt, what the damp grass that stretched down them felt under the cold rain.

I felt like I *was* the vineyard.

My mind floated deeper out of my relaxed body and into the dark fields that I knew so well; the fields that waited for me to see them when the sun rose and the light illuminated the glistening dampness of it all.

I sighed in sheer peace at the fact that when the sun was to come up, I would still be sitting right here, looking out onto the land that could now be seen so clearly and I wouldn't want to be anywhere else.

Even if it was a crisp, cold, dismal day, the difference in the light when the sun first reaches up in the sky and shines down onto the green, compared to the anticipating darkness I now sat in, was enough to give the day and the atmosphere the impression of being light and sunny and warm.

I pictured myself lying on the grass of one of the paths with my shirt off, feeling the wet grass under my skin – fresh and crisp and cold. I would get up and the dampness would drip down my back and onto the rim of my trousers and I would feel it seeping through. It would be uncomfortable, but the fact I would wish I hadn't done it, the fact I would wish I'd stayed standing up, would be life affirming.

It's joyous to do something you know you're going to regret.

I'd walk back wet to the mansion and get changed and then get on with my day's work on the land; I'd get back on with my life; my whole life.

I was so lost in the peace of the moment that I had almost forgotten what had been bothering me for the past few months. It was only when out of nowhere the thought came back to me, that I was able to appreciate the brief time it had slipped away. Why is it, one can never appreciate solitude until it is too late?

I had been living with a murderer and the worst kind of murderer; a man who had killed his own wife and son.

How could I have gotten Bernard so wrong? How did I see him as this frail, kind-hearted old man? I could still hardly believe it; I was still in denial, disbelief. When I pictured Bernard's face I saw it differently to how I used to see it. I used to see it as loving and vulnerable, father like; now I saw it as dark and evil, with bloodshot eyes. I couldn't help but envision him scratching those engravings on to the gravestones, probably using the same knife as he used to put the people underneath.

But then I couldn't help but picture him lying in his bed the night he died, his weak, weak voice saying, 'Thank you, son.' The two visions just didn't seem like they were of the same person.

The ghostly howl of an owl blew through the dark air around me and woke me up from my deep, disturbing thoughts.

Thankfully, I was back on the rocking chair. The rain continued to drizzle down from the open black sky and as I ran my hand over my dressing gown it was soaked, but the inside however, was still as dry and warm and snug as ever.

146

As I sat, trying to focus on the here and now, the wind and the rain and not about Bernard whose name alone sent shivers down my spine, I wasn't quite sure how I felt. I let out a shudder from the cold. I was either in total and utter peace, completely comfortable with where I was right now, pleased that I had got here and not fallen victim to myself or the murderer I had been living with or maybe, I thought, just maybe, I felt a sense of terror surrounding me, as if the shadows of this places past were coming back to haunt me.

It was somewhat enlightening to realise that sometimes one is incapable of determining how one feels, or even knowing if it is good or bad.

However, I soon realised which one I felt, when the cold wind settled and a warmth blew gently through the air; and then, even feeling the heat, I shuddered again.

****

John had now taken full charge of the vineyard. He was a natural. Although however pleased I was, I hoped he didn't share many of the same genes with his father.

The harvest had gone extremely well and I had been right about my prediction. I thought the wine would do well with investors, as they would believe that it would be the last good vintage and it did. In fact it was Belet's most financially successful harvest ever.

The idea that the market looked upon Bernard as some sort of legend in the winemaking world angered me as much as it sickened me, but then again how could I judge people for not knowing somebody. Just a few months ago, I was ready to start calling him 'dad.'

I didn't think about the business side of things as I walked the field's alone, plucking deadheads off the grape bushes and snipping weeds off the grassy ground. For the first month or so, after playing such an important role in such a big business event, I had to make a conscious effort to block all the numbers and the people and the dealings out of my mind and focus on the land. However, by now I had grown use to the isolation; the peace I had come here for in the first place.

When I did stop and look back on the harvest, I saw it as a mere hiccough in my journey, something small and insignificant I had to overcome, just like the struggle to get on the ferry back in Dover; difficult at the time, but small and insignificant none the less and in hindsight, tiny in comparison to the grand scheme of things. This was a journey of my heart and I had finally managed to reach the place I had come here for; the grass under my feet in the middle of the vineyard with no one else around.

The idea sometimes came over me that I still didn't know where I truly was. I had been so sure about Bernard; I had been so sure that I had found my place even when I was living with him and look how wrong I was. 'How could I be so sure I had found my place now? How could I be a hundred percent that John wasn't a secret serial killer or that the vineyard was due to be closed down and turned into flats?'

No.

I knew I couldn't think like that. Bernard's case was a one off, rare, uncommon. John was a normal person and the vineyard had a contract attached to it that it wouldn't be redeveloped unless the owner agreed to it. Everything was fine.

Everything was fine.

I didn't speak to John much. Partly it was down to the fact that he was always so caught up in paperwork, busy with drawing up expansion plans for the vineyard. It was easy to tell that he felt he had something to prove to me, to himself and to the ancestors he never knew.

But to tell the truth it was also because of the fact that I wanted so much to just be alone. John being here meant that I could be and I wanted his feature in my life to be one that allowed me to fulfil my dream.

I had never had many friends in my life apart from of course Eric and a few others and I could have become good friends with John, but to me, the idea of solitude seemed infinitely more enticing and I couldn't have friendship stand in my way.

In my eyes, as I stood in the middle of the crisp cold vineyard, the sky bright and open above me, all there was, was the land and me, and that is all there ever needed to be.

****

The wind blew with quite a force all around me, it ran through my hair like icy water; my face stung.

I was walking the pathways in the middle of the vineyard, one of many points where every horizon was nothing but grape bushes and sky.

Every vine needed to be carefully checked over several times throughout the course of the year to ensure they were healthy and not spreading diseases to the other vines. If they were found to be unhealthy or diseased, I would have to cut them out by the root and dispose of them. But even checking each vine just three times a year, it was still enough to keep me busy all day every day.

I didn't get bored or maybe I did, but my boredom was disguised as something else, relaxation maybe. Plucking the grape bushes filled me with the same feeling as lying on a deckchair in the sun would; boredom, but good boredom, the sort of boredom one would get from doing little out of choice, not out of duty.

Only about one in a thousand vines would be in poor shape, and it felt satisfying to know that that low statistic that made the job easier was down to the fact that I did the job efficiently. This meant that there was no point in dragging around the digging tools when having the need for them was unlikely. Instead, I carried a notepad around in my coat pocket so that if I did find any vine that needed my attention, I could record its location and come straight back to it with the tools. I knew the vineyard like the back of my hand now.

The sky was a solid sheet of light grey. The land, a dull green and brown spread, rolled over a hard earth. However, even in the dull atmosphere, there was a warm light inside me, one that shone so brightly in my mind and in my soul I could almost see it illuminating the fields before me.

As the wind settled, my mind started to wander back to a day a long, long time ago. I must have been about ten or eleven at the time. It felt like another lifetime ago.

My childhood home had a large garden, about a quarter of an acre and the wild bushes that lined the back, backed on to fields.

My dad had cut a small hole in the mesh fence so that whenever we wanted to go for walks through the fields, we didn't have to walk all the way to the main entrance about half a mile away; instead, we could just crawl through the bushes at the back of our garden. I remember him covering it with leaves on either side and my mum standing ten feet away saying, 'Are you sure we should be doing this?' 'It will be fine!' my dad had proclaimed. 'If you say so, dear,' my mum had answered unconvincingly.

My mum had told me that when I was a bit older, I could go through the hole on my own and explore the fields as long as I didn't go too far and always made a mental note of where I had gone so that I could find my way back. 'Make note of any landmarks,' she told me. I'd asked her what 'landmarks' were, and she told me that they were 'any funny looking trees or anything that looked out of place or noticeable; things that I would remember by seeing, even if I had since forgotten.'

The next day I asked her if I was old enough; both her and my dad laughed and told me, 'not yet.'

The following day I asked again. My mum told me that she would tell me when I was old enough.

I restrained from asking the next day but I couldn't get the thought of it out of my mind. To me it was like seeing a door half open and not being able to walk through it; a door to a room that I had been in many times but never been able to truly explore. My mum had told me that I could 'explore' the fields. Every time I walked through them with them, all we would do is walk and talk and stand still every time the sun came out from behind the clouds. But on my own I could really go out and discover them. I could run to the highest hill and see the view or crawl down to the deepest ditch and dig down further to find if there were any caves or gold.

A day later I couldn't help but ask again. 'Please can I go through the hole?' 'No,' my mum replied strictly, fed up with my persistence.

What my parents didn't understand was the feeling I had. I think I was only seven at the time and obviously too young to go out on my own, but I felt like I had to. They thought I wanted to go out to play and have fun but to me, it didn't feel like fun, it felt like it was just something I needed to do.

Even I didn't know at the time why it was that I felt the way I did. It wasn't that I didn't want to be at home; I had a good home life as a child, there was just something inside me telling me I needed to go through that hole and into the fields. I suppose it was instinct.

But, being a seven year old, with the help of my favourite cartoons and toys, I soon forgot all about the hole. Amazingly, looking back, even when we went for walks through the fields, which I think my parents avoided for several months, I didn't remember. It must have been a shame for them that for so long they never even got to use the hole my dad had cut to get into the fields so that I wouldn't start up again; we would always walk round the road way.

Then, one morning, about three or four years later, my mum came into my room and called my name. I looked over from the top of my bunk bed. 'What is the furthest thing you can remember?' she'd said. 'Umm,' I'd replied. My mum looked at me. 'Do you remember when you were seven years old and Dad cut a hole in our garden fence?' My face must have looked puzzled because at that point I didn't remember. She smiled. 'So that we could sneak into the field from our garden instead of walking round the road to get there?' I must have still looked puzzled. 'You were desperate to go through it on your own, to explore? You asked me again and again and I told you that you could when you were older?' 'I can't remember, mum.' I had replied, a little confused. 'Well, anyway,' my mum began, 'you are old enough now.' I smiled, but I was still confused.

Later that day, my mum told me to put my shoes and coat on and took me out the back door. There was a real chill in the air that day, the sort of chill that goes straight through you, whatever you're wearing. My mum wrapped her arm around me to keep me warm. 'I think you'll remember it when you see it,' she said to me.

We clambered through the opening into the bushes and stopped at the mesh fence. There was a big pile of rotten leaves and shrubbery piled up against a bit of it and my mum began to brush it away. Then the top of the hole became visible and I saw through to the green fields on the other side.

It started to come back to me slowly and then all of a sudden out of nowhere, I remembered everything.

'I remember! I remember!' I shouted and my mum laughed. She stroked my hair and kissed me on the top of my head and when she leant back up and I saw her, she seemed more like she had been crying than laughing, like my happiness meant so much more to her than I realised at that age.

'We can finally use this to get to the fields!' She laughed. 'We've always gone the road way because we thought if we went through here with you, you would start asking to go through it on your own again and we had to wait till you were old enough.'

'I don't think I should have gone through to the fields on my own at seven, mum.' I said.

'No,' she smiled. 'But you're old enough and sensible enough now, aren't you?'

'Definitely!' I answered. 'I will look for the landmarks wherever I go so I can *never* get lost!'

My mum gave a look of shock and amazement. 'You remembered what I told you?'

'Yes.'

'Oh, James,' she cried, and she hugged me tightly by the hole in the mesh fence in the bushes at the back of our garden, warm and snug and sheltered from the cold wind.

We went back inside and my mum gave me my rucksack. She told me that she had put some tissues, some plasters and a pen and paper in there in case I needed to record any landmarks so that I didn't forget my way back home. She also gave me another pen in case the first one ran out.

Then she told me to close my eyes and put my hands out, so I did.

'You got me a present!' I shouted happily and I felt her put something hard and heavy in my hands.

'Open your eyes!' She said.

I kept my eyes closed for a few moments, excited about what it could be. I was expecting a new toy or maybe a new pair of trainers but it didn't feel like the right shape. I opened my eyes, and saw this strange yellow device with a big stick sticking out of it and buttons all over it. I looked at my mum, as if to ask what it was.

She smiled. 'It's called a Walkie Talkie,' she told me. 'I've bought myself one as well.'

I turned the thing over in my hands, trying to work it out and what you were meant to do with it.

She explained to me what it was and showed me how to use it. Every time she noticed my attention was wondering off, she nudged me and said that she couldn't stress enough how important it was. 'And you can't lose it,' she told me, 'not only is it very expensive but it is very, very important you keep it on you at all times when you're out on your own. Do you understand?'

'Yes.' I did.

'Now, I will always have mine on me when you are out on your own, so if you ever need to contact me I will be right here.'

'Can I go and explore now please, Mum,' I asked.

'Yes,' she said and she began to push me encouragingly towards the door. 'Go! Before the weather gets any worse!' she said as I walked out the door and onto the patio. 'Go and explore!' Then, as I ran onto the grass I heard her faint, rather distant voice, but I knew she was shouting, 'Don't forget to keep your Walkie Talkie on you at all times!'

'I won't!' I shouted, turning back, but hardly stopping and half tripping as I raced to the hole I'd unknowingly waited almost four years to crawl through.

"Come straight back if you get cold!" I heard the faintest voice from far behind me.

"Okay!" I shouted back, knowing I'd almost definitely not be heard.

It was difficult to crawl through. I had to be extremely careful not to scratch myself on the roughly cut metal meshing of the fence as I dragged my body through. But I managed.

I picked myself up off the wet grass and looked up at the fields before me. They spread out as far as the eye could see. The sky was a harsh grey and the cold rain was bucketing down from all angles in the ferocious wind. I felt so small and insignificant, so vulnerable.

All of a sudden there was a huge gust of wind and the rain hit me at the exact same time from the same direction, nearly knocking me back into the bushes. I crouched down to try to avoid it but it felt like there was no escape. I turned around and looked back at the hole I had just crawled through. I could see the dry earth of the sheltered bushes through it, inviting me in.

I did think for a moment about crawling back through but then something suddenly hit me and this time it wasn't the wind or the rain. It was a voice that seemed to come from the hole. I couldn't hear the voice, instead I could feel it, as if it was actually coming from inside me. It was my mum's voice.

'Go,' she kept saying, that and nothing else. 'Go,' 'go,' 'go.'

So I pushed myself up against the howling wind, my coat dripping down to my trousers with rain and I turned to face the horizon.

There I stood for a second, fearing what lay in front of me, but knowing I couldn't return right then to what lay behind me or even stay where I was.

So, with trembling legs both cold and nervous and a body shaking like a rag doll in the heavy wind, with uncertainty, I walked.

After half an hour, the rain and the wind having subsided, I felt a vibration coming from my rucksack so I took it off and saw that the Walkie Talkie was ringing. I answered it and I heard my mum's voice asking if I was okay and how far I had gone. It was reassuring to hear her voice and to know that I wasn't alone. I told her that I was fine and that I had walked miles and miles. She told me to remember that however far I walk, I would have to walk that same distance back so don't tire myself out too much, and also to make sure that I got back for lunch which was in two hours. I was wearing a kid's watch so I knew the time.

When the conversation and the call ended a thought suddenly came over me as if from nowhere. I had wanted the freedom of being on my own in the fields and I should be brave enough to be truly alone. In my eyes I was all grown up and almost had something to prove. But more than that, I just had a feeling inside me that with my Walkie Talkie I wasn't truly free.

With guilt and fear running through my mind, knowing that my mum would more than likely find out and have a big go at me when I returned, I pulled the Walkie Talkie out from my bag and switched it off, just as she had earlier shown me how to and told me not to do.

The second I heard the buzz that indicated it was off, sounding out of place in the natural place full of natural sounds like birds and rain, I felt instantly free. I felt like the chains around me that I had only just began to feel had broken, like the door to the cage had just opened and I was free to walk out, free to walk alone into the distance.

The more free I felt, the less free I felt like I had been.

I didn't realise at the time how much of an impact this moment would have on my life. The fact I felt so at peace, so free and had such belonging alone on the land, made every day spent anywhere else, anywhere within the confines of society, made me feel the exact opposite; trapped, anxious and as if I didn't belong.

But I don't believe for a second that this moment was the sole origin of my lifelong demons. I think it was just the first time I really realised I had them.

It amazes me to this day how big I thought those fields were. To me, they spread into every distance and as I ran through them, it felt like they would never end. It felt like the town I lived in and the city that surrounded it was just a tiny speck in the middle of the fields and the land stretched out to the edges of the world. But as I grew up, I realised that all they were, were a collection of five fields and a small woodland in the middle, only two miles all in all, surrounded on every side by roads and houses.

Years later, after my parents had passed away and the house had been sold to new owners, I had to go round to sign some documents. It brought back a lot of memories of my childhood and was a very emotional visit. They let me have a wonder through the garden on my own, so I went to the bushes and looked for the hole. It had been repaired and instead of a view through to the fields on the other side, all I could see was shiny new meshing, as if my memories had been varnished over.

I remember so, so clearly, standing in those bushes on that frosty winters' day; I was about twenty-three at the time, looking back at my childhood, my demons as prevalent in the forefront of my mind as they had ever been. I could hear my mum's voice and I could feel her wrapping her arms around me to keep me warm. I missed her and my dad so very much at that point in my life; I still do, but my grief has long ago settled down to a fond memory of them.

I remember standing there, knowing that I needed to go back to the house that was no longer mine before the new owners became suspicious of my whereabouts. But there was something stopping me from leaving the bushes, something that was telling me I couldn't go back to the life I had dreaded living since my school days. The bushes sheltered me from that life and I couldn't bear the idea of walking back into the garden and back into the house; I couldn't bear the idea of facing my life.

Then I heard my mum's voice again and I can still hear it to this day when I look back on that moment. 'Go.' 'Go.' 'Go.' Her voice kept saying.

But as I looked at the new meshing covering where the hole used to be, I noticed how no one would have ever guessed that it used to be a secret passageway to the fields.

And now, it was no more than another wall, another barricade.

I remember how the wind blew so ferociously as I forced myself to clamber back out of the bushes and into the garden.

My mind brought me back to the here and now, back to September on the vineyard, the cold wind blowing through my hair and my face stinging in the cold.

I continued to walk down the paths checking every grape bush thoroughly to ensure they were all perfect.

I stood back up after checking the underneath part of one of the vines and as I did so, I felt a warmth on my face and a light in the corner of my eye. I looked up at the sky and saw that behind a grey cloud, the sun had started to ever so slightly come out.

I was able to look at it with squinted eyes, as it was so slight and as I did, as I felt it arming up my body as if from the inside, I couldn't help but smile.

It was like a speck of shimmering gold in the middle of an ocean of grey.

Fifteen

"Let's go out," I heard John say from across the dining room table.

John was the sort of person you could sit with, saying nothing and it would not be at all awkward. The first time I met him and in the weeks that followed, he was different. It was hard to hold a conversation with him and he rarely made eye contact. I could see it wasn't because he was shy but because the whole situation was a difficult one. But after getting to know him, he felt comfortable with me and I felt comfortable with him and I saw him in a completely different light.

However, over the past few months, I had been extremely hostile. Of course it was because I wanted it to be just me and the land; I felt like the more cold I was with John and the quieter I was around him, the more isolated I would feel, and that's exactly what I wanted.

But John was adamant on remaining my friend. He never gave up trying to engage in conversation, not because the silence was awkward, but because he just wanted to talk, wanted to continue bonding. I understood this completely. I myself had never had many friends and if I met somebody I got along with, I felt it was vital to connect with them so that I didn't lose them. I knew John was the same as he spoke and spoke and asked question after question, ignoring my disinterest, pretending that he thought my mind was in the room not on the vineyard, even though I know he knew it wasn't, and tonight was no exception.

"Oh, come on James," he said.

I looked up from my plate at his trying eyes. "Where?" I said coldly, with a slight guilt hidden beneath my words.

"There is a club I used to go to quite a bit in town," he said, enthusiastically.

"What sort of club?" I asked.

John gave me a look.

I realised what sort of club he meant.

"No," I said.

"James, may I remind you, because I think you sometimes forget, you're not married to the vines." John didn't smile. He seemed a bit annoyed.

"I know I'm not," I replied; nothing more needed to be said. It wasn't even about my relationship with the land, I just didn't agree with paying to watch desperate women strip.

"Somewhere else then!" John said.

"I suppose we could go somewhere."

"I think I know a place you'll like." John smiled.

I looked at him suspiciously.

"It's called Le Saxophone Ivre." When John spoke French his accent was indistinguishable to that of a Frenchman. "It means, 'The drunken Saxophone,'" he continued, "it's a jazz club."

My eyes must have lit up. "Where is it?" I asked, noticeably interested.

John smiled widely, looking like he had achieved what he had set out to achieve. It may not have been his first choice, but he had made me come round.

"It's in Bordeaux," he replied.

****

Later that evening, as the overhanging leaves rustled violently against the window in the wind and the dark vineyard seemed to be howling at me through the walls, I started to get ready to go out.

I put on my shirt and trousers and then my blazer and looked in the mirror, letting out a small sigh. It was the first time I'd worn that suit since arriving in Belet and it brought back a few rather unpleasant memories of claustrophobia and distress.

I walked over to the curtain as the wind outside screamed at the glass, and put my forehead against it. It sounded like there was a wolf just the other side. I was deep, deep in thought; well, not so much thought, but my mind was a long way away from the present.

There was a loud knocking at my bedroom door.

I jumped back away from the window.

"Ready yet?" I heard through the closed door. "Taxi's here."

"Yes. Yes," I said, grabbing my wallet and my key from the bedside cabinet and walking over to the door. I opened it and saw John. He was wearing a fancy suit I had never seen before; jet black with small gold markings on the shoulders and shiny, shiny black shoes, with about a two inch heel.

He looked at me and I could see it was almost in disapproval, but then he smiled.

"Let's go," he said, and we walked downstairs. I grabbed my dark brown shoes from the shelf near the door and we walked outside.

I could see the taxi waiting for us; the taxi driver oblivious to the trail he had caused on the sandy path. I looked up at the vineyard behind and then left to the shed and the small flickering light on top which looked warm in the freezing late night chill. I shuddered as the breeze hit my face.

"Come on!" shouted John, getting into the taxi.

I didn't answer; I just turned and bent down, to lock the big black front door. It was rare to lock the door as usually, even when we were both out on the vineyard, shutting it seemed enough, however as we were both leaving the premises, I thought it was a good idea.

As I turned the key, I heard the crunching cogs inside the lock clicking shut, followed by a rather heavy thudding sound inside the door; it reminded me of a noise I'd heard somewhere before but as I walked towards the taxi and for the duration of the ride into Bordeaux, as John tried to engage me in conversation, I couldn't for the life of me think where.

****

I didn't know what was more consuming; the music on the stage or the loud, inaudible murmur of the rest of the room.

From the outside, the jazz club was nothing to get excited about. In fact, it was nothing at all, just a small door that looked like it had been forced in between two shops.

However, after entering and walking down not one but two flights of stairs and through another door, you were suddenly transported into a completely different place.

Even standing at the bottom of the stairs I could hear the beating of the noise vibrating through the thick wooden door and when I opened it, it hit me. I had to pause for a moment so that my head wouldn't burst before braving it inside.

Having been in the club for an hour now, I had grown used to the noise, the flashing lights, the clinking of the glasses and the overwhelming talking and laughter. I had grown used to it but I still didn't feel comfortable with it. It just felt too much.

I just sat there, taking it all in, trying to feel like I was a part of it, forcing myself to believe that I was right there in the noise, in the club but it was difficult.

John was the other side of the room talking to a couple of women both wearing similar sparkling dresses covered in sequins, glimmering like diamonds in the lights. I looked down and through the heads bobbing up and down across the room, I could see their dresses only came down to the very top of their legs.

I felt myself staring at their legs, as they leant to pick up their drinks from the bar and danced around on the spot. I knew I was doing it, but with the noise blaring in my ears and the frantic huddles of people singing and dancing all around me, smashing champagne glasses together, I felt so out of my body I didn't care.

I forced my eyes away, reminding myself of my morals, forcing, forcing myself to be in my body.

I focused on the instruments on the stage. There were four men. The one in the middle at the front played the saxophone with all his might. His face was red. He looked like he was about to drop but he blew and blew and blew. Behind him, one plucked away madly at his cello, another smashed at a set of drums and the last one on the left strummed calmly at his base guitar, one smooth strum every two or three seconds. His eyes looked like they weren't there, to be honest, he looked as high as a kite and I imagined I must have looked the same.

The only difference was that he was more than likely high on one or more substances whereas I was high on something else, something much more internal, making me feel like I wasn't really there.

I closed my eyes. The noise grew even louder, even more unbearable. I kept them shut for a few moments just trying to accept it, but I couldn't, so I opened them again.

I looked back over at John. One hand was clasped around his glass at his mouth, as he glugged down some gold coloured spirit, the other was on one of the women's legs, just where her dress fell to. They were all laughing and hopping up and down to the beat of the drums. I saw his face fall in to the woman's face so they were nearly touching and his fingers start to reach up inside the material of her dress.

I looked the other way.

There was a large gathering of people, there must have been about twelve of them, all laughing together, each one seeming like they were trying to be louder than the person next to them. They all seemed to be dancing together in one big, chaotic mess.

I gulped down my double whisky and stood up. I'd had quite a bit to drink. I felt myself falling back onto my chair as if the room and everything in it, all the lights and the noise were falling away from me, falling away from my senses, as if I was falling out of sync with myself. I didn't know if I was more drunk from the alcohol, the environment or my thoughts, but I just about managed to stay standing.

I started to walk over to the bar and peered over at where John had been standing but I couldn't see him. I looked over all the people in the way and they moved back and forward in and out of my line of vision.

Then I saw him. His hands were touching each other behind the woman's back, pressing his body towards hers and they were kissing deeply, seemingly to the music. The other women seemed to have gone.

"Double whisky," I said to the barman when I reached the bar, pressing my hands against the surface to hold myself up.

He turned around and shoved some ice cubes in the glass then poured it out. He put it on the counter and I slid a twenty pound note across to him; as I glugged it down, the ice smashing against my teeth. I heard it, but I didn't feel it.

"Same again," I said, as he took the note.

He looked at me and then turned around and put a glass on the back surface of the bar. He tipped in the ice and then the whisky and turned around and put it on the table in front of me, giving me another disapproving look as he did so.

I just looked back, vacantly, and picked up the glass, taking a big sip as I turned around to walk back to the chair, not even waiting for the change.

Then, as the room fell away from me, I had no choice but to lean back against the bar, which had somehow become about two feet away from me. As I leant back, I fell and hit my back and the back of my head against the wooden side, dropping my glass. It shattered into a thousand tiny pieces on the floor beside me.

I found myself a second later, when the blackness around me faded back into the room, on the floor, uncomfortably leaning against the bar. The music was blaring and peoples' legs danced all around me as if I had sunk down into the floor of the club.

People stepped over me, hardly noticing I was there.

I put one weak hand on the floor and stumbled onto my front, then lifted myself up using the top of the bar as support. After holding my balance for a second, not wanting to fall again, I pushed myself slowly away from the bar and started carefully making my way towards the exit. I looked over to where John had been, as however much I didn't want to intrude on his situation, I needed to tell him that I needed to go and I would see him back at the house the next day.

But as I searched for him with my eyes through the crowd, he was nowhere to be seen and neither was the woman he was somewhat groping.

I just walked to the door and as I put my hand on it to push it open, I noticed the door to the women's toilets closing and a man's hand I recognised on its edge pulling it shut.

I became aware of how little expression I was showing despite the thoughts in my head, which were a complete blur underneath all the alcohol that swam around my body and my head. I pushed the heavy door open with what felt like all my strength and stumbled out into the much-needed quiet of the stairs.

I fell forward and caught my balance against the rusty banister. I felt the alcohol coming up my oesophagus and I thought for a second I was going to be sick, but I held it in and without taking my hands off the banister for a second, I stumbled up the two flights of stairs to the front door.

Out into the cold night I walked and I breathed in the crisp air deeply, letting it fill and cleanse my lungs. I could feel it was cold, but my body felt warm on the inside. All I was really aware of was the overwhelming dark. The lights of the other bars and clubs along the strip shone brightly, but all they seemed to do was accentuate the vast blackness of the sky and the air that surrounded me.

I was well aware of how drunk I was; I felt terribly dizzy and light headed, I wasn't in control of my body at all. Even my mind felt drenched in the alcohol, like my mind had drowned in the many glasses of whisky I had been glugging down throughout the course of the night.

But even in this desperate state, even with my brain not working properly, not thinking straight, I could still feel something inside. My brain somehow still managed to hold one thought in, that became clearer than ever in the deep pool of alcohol inside me.

I could feel it, as strong as it had ever been, vibrating against the very foundations of my soul, banging, banging, banging against the windows of the room it had been hiding in, deep inside my head.

The thought that even in Belet, I still didn't belong.

****

I can't remember how long it was since I'd left the jazz club. I knew I needed to phone for a taxi but I just wanted to walk for a while. I wasn't even thinking about sobering up, I was just appreciating the fresh air.

The strip of bars and clubs had since disappeared into the distance and the road had turned into more of a deserted 'A' road that seemed to lead out of town. There were two lanes on either side, separated by a short concrete wall in the middle and on my side there was a pavement, separated from the fast road by another long straight wall about four feet high. To my right, as I walked, there was nothing but open space and behind that, industrial estate after industrial estate; graffiti over almost every wall.

Only the odd car sped past way past the speed limit. Its headlights would light up the otherwise dark area for a brief few moments before it disappeared into the distance.

Lampposts lined the streets but half of them weren't working. Cat's eyes lined the middle of the roads so the cars could see where they were going, but obviously not very well, as every car that went past had their headlights on full beam. I could see the cars on the other side of the concrete wall coming towards me and every time they did, it dazzled me and my eyes pounded from the bright lights.

There was a bridge in the distance that I seemed to be heading towards. There were long steps that led up and over the 'A' road. It looked derelict, like one shouldn't dare walk over it.

I planned to.

I was starting to get a bit chilly as my feelings were coming back to me and I was beginning to sober up, but only very slightly. I was still very much under the influence.

I reached the bridge and walked up the steps to the top and then followed it right until I was standing thirty feet above the road.

Something made me stop walking.

I walked over to the edge of the bridge and put my hands on the railing.

Peering over, I could see the tarmac far below me, straight down, nothing in between it and me. Then I saw in the top of my line of vision, the full beam headlights from a car speeding towards me. It made me quiver as I watched it storm straight underneath where I was standing and I turned suddenly to see it disappearing into the darkness.

I turned back to the road over the railings, just taking in how high up I was and how far the drop was.

I felt my hands tightening around the top bar of the railing. I rose on to my tiptoes and put my weight on my hands. The railing was brown and rusting. My abdomen fell slowly against it and I leant ever so slightly forward.

Then ever so slightly more.

Then slightly, just slightly more, and I felt my toes come off the ground.

Suddenly I felt my body topple forward, like when you're falling asleep and you jerk awake or when you feel yourself about to fall back on a chair.

For a second everything left my mind, all my worries, all my fears, all my demons. I felt then as sober as ever.

Every muscle in my arms suddenly tightened and my grip around the bar became so firm I could almost hear the skin between my thumb and index finger splitting and my knuckles cracking.

But someone must have been on my side that night because I somehow managed to catch my balance and stop myself from tumbling over the railing to my death.

After my feet were back on the ground, I pushed down on them feeling the concrete under my shoes. I was still holding on to the railing, frightened to take my hands off. I felt a sudden rush of instability come over me and every muscle in my body felt completely weak and lifeless, as if I was made of jelly, and I crumbled to the ground against the railing.

Then I felt an overwhelming sickness come over me and I felt a burning in my throat. Then I was sick over the railing and I watched as it dribbled down the rusty metal to the ground of the bridge, saliva streaming down from my mouth, forming a line from my face to the ground.

I breathed out deeply, wiped my mouth and closed my eyes, an overwhelming tiredness coming over me. I felt like lying down but knew it wasn't a good idea. With my eyes closed I felt sick again; I felt like I was moving along as fast as the cars I could hear every so often below me and spinning around, I felt uneasy with my eyes closed, like the ground of the bridge had become wafer thin.

I needed to get off, and fast.

I pulled myself up and without letting go of the railing I ran uncomfortably, straight to the steps, feeling the rust splintering like frail wood under my hands as I slid both of them along the bar to my right.

I walked carefully down the long steps, still not taking my hands off the railing.

It was only when I got to the bottom and saw a small road leading away from the 'A' road did I realise that in my mad rush to get off the bridge, I had walked the wrong way; not the way I had come.

I suddenly realised how drunk I was still, as I looked down the road and felt myself falling slightly forward, unable to stand up straight and still.

Knowing that I should go back the way I came, I turned to go back onto the bridge, but all of a sudden a horrible feeling came over me. I couldn't face walking back up there. I looked up to the top of it from where only a few minutes earlier I had almost plummeted, and I felt myself almost throw up again.

I turned to my right and looked down the small road as the noise of a car whizzed past behind me and without thinking, I started to walk down it.

'I'll just find a road name and then call a taxi,' I thought to myself, as I walked further down this dark road, lit only by the odd lamppost. There were high fences on either side and behind that, thick bushes that I couldn't see beyond.

Then after a few minutes I saw a building on my left. It was concrete with large thin windows and a big weak looking glass door. It looked very much out of place mainly because of the fact that all the lights were on.

It was the middle of the night, I was far away from any bar and this place, whatever it was, was open.

As I walked towards it I could see white tiles lining the walls through the windows and when I got to the door I noticed it was slightly ajar.

I cautiously stepped towards it and pushed it slightly open, incredibly artificial white light pouring into my eyes.

An intense smell of chlorine filled my nose. It was strange and extremely unexpected.

I stepped back almost in shock and pulled the door ajar again, before walking over to the big window and looking through.

Sure enough, there before me was a swimming pool.

I could see through the window, the old white tiles lining the floor and the walls around it and a door beyond that with the signs: 'Men's Vestiaire' and 'Women's Vestiaire.' I presumed they were changing rooms.

I stepped back away from the window. It was so quiet down this road. Even in the middle of the night it was noticeably dead. It just gave the impression of even being this empty in the day.

I walked back over to the door, pushed it open and walked through into an old hallway with two vending machines against the wall that backed onto the road I had just come in from. One had drinks and chocolates, but the money slot looked broken and the machine was half empty; the other was full of goggles, flippers and swimming hats.

I had never seen a vending machine with swimming equipment in before, only ever food and drinks. It was a first for me.

Everything was still spinning slightly; I felt much less drunk than I had done earlier but since entering the hallway, the bright white lights had made me feel a bit ill, and it was extremely hot and humid. The sudden temperature change made me feel extra hot and uncomfortable.

I walked over to the door on my left and peered through the glass strip to see the swimming pool. Then I pushed the door slightly open to have a closer look and a wave of heat suddenly hit me.

I wanted to cool down. I hadn't been swimming in many, many years and I knew now didn't seem like the ideal time. My shirt was beginning to dampen from sweat giving me an unpleasant chill, but overall I felt hot.

The idea of jumping in the pool was so enticing and the more I thought about it, the more it began to override my common sense; the cool water all over me. I would hold my breath and sink under the surface. It would sober me up if anything.

I closed the door, cutting off the wave of heat and looked back at the vending machine with equipment in. I walked over to it and looked at the goggles, then at the slot. It looked fully intact.

'Five Euros' it had written on it next to one of the pairs of goggles that appeared to be nearly falling out of its slot.

I got out my wallet and emptied the coins into my hand. One of the coins slipped through my fingers and rolled straight under the machine. I didn't register what it was but it looked golden to me.

I counted the coins as I put them into the slot of the vending machine and when I'd put the fifth one in, I pressed on the button for goggles and they dropped out.

I pushed up the black plastic flap and pulled them out. They weren't in any packet at all, just the goggles and that was it. I tried them on for size and they were a perfect fit.

Leaving them on, I took my jacket off and put it down on the floor by my feet and then unbuttoned my shit and ripped it off, putting that on top of my jacket. Then I rolled my trouser legs up to just above my knees and scrunched them up higher so that they stuck. I took my watch off and as I did, I looked at it in the white light of the room, having not been able to read the time in the dark all evening and all night. It was ten minutes to four.

I picked up my shirt and jacket, scrunching them up in my hand and walked through the door to the swimming pool, the wave of heat hitting me again but making me feel good as I knew I was about to cool down.

The pool looked like it was fifty metres in length and at the far end I saw a lifeguard sitting high up on a chair. I couldn't see him from the window or the door. I looked over to him as I walked over to the pool, hoping he wouldn't tell me I couldn't go in, but I don't think he even noticed I was there. He looked like he was half falling asleep, leaning to one side on the arm of the chair as if it was the only thing preventing him from falling off.

I shoved my clothes and watch down on the deckchair and took my shoes and socks off, before walking over to the edge of the pool, the heat and humidity consuming my body.

Glancing over at the depth sign, I could see it said two metres. I tried to calculate it into feet, something I could usually do exactly in a second, but in my tired, still drunken, rather ill state, I had no chance. All I knew was that it was deeper than I was tall; but I would have known that a few moments later anyway.

I felt the goggles were still tight against my face and suddenly remembered something my mum had told me years ago; that, 'one shouldn't jump into water with goggles on or your eyes will pop out.' It sounded like an old wives tale to me.

I took a deep breath in and felt like the humidity was hardly filling my lungs, and then I jumped.

A rush of cold came over me as I sank down, feeling the water going into my nose and ears. For about two or three seconds I was fully under, my feet just about touching the bottom, the water about a foot or so above my head, then the water pulled me up to the surface and my head bobbed up. My ears popped the water out and I opened my eyes and only then realised that they had been closed during my jump, even though under the goggles they needn't have been. The water ran down my face and I coughed the taste of chlorine out my mouth. My hair was drenched forward over my forehead and was on the tip of my goggles so I brushed it back with both hands, falling back slightly under the surface so I felt the water flow into my ears again. I caught the side and pulled myself forward towards it.

I was starting to grow used to the cold temperature of the water but I could tell it was a pretty cold pool.

I turned around using the side of the pool to push myself against and my feet as support and then made myself sink down underneath. In one motion I went under the water and pushed off the side with both feet, propelling myself like a dart into the open water.

175

It rushed past me, feeling like I was staying still and it was everything else going past. I felt refreshed, but quite light headed and faint. My legs began to kick frantically and my arms began to naturally do a mixture of front crawl and doggy paddle.

Something made me want to stay under the water for as long as possible, so I did. I felt my muscles start rapidly tiring and my lungs beginning to need air, more and more every second, so I came up and took in a deep breath, snorting up masses of water in the process. I felt it going straight down my windpipe and into my lungs as I went back under the surface and continued to flap my limbs about and push myself forward.

Quite soon after, I started to desperately need air again so I came up again and tried to breathe just through my mouth but it didn't work and I felt another stream of water and the taste of chlorine go down. I went back under and continued to swim.

Before I expected it, I reached the end and I pulled myself up against the side. I breathed in and out deeply and as I came round from the breathlessness, I looked up and around and saw the lifeguard on the high chair. I could see he was awake but only just; he was leaning on the armrest uncomfortably, his eyes only slightly open, looking like he was in a complete daze. It looked like he still hadn't noticed my presence but he must have done.

When my breathing began to slow, I put my head under the water and pushed off with my legs much more slowly than the first time.

As I began to attempt breast stroke, I noticed the white tiles on the floor of the pool. Each one was about half a foot square and they spread symmetrically across the entire pool.

I came up for air and looking for a second across the surface, I noticed I had hardly moved anywhere. I went back under.

The tiles were separated by light brown lines stretching throughout, crisscrossing through the white. Staring at the line and following it as I slowly swam above it, I felt like I was floating a mile up above a pathway that appeared small and thin far below me.

I came up for air.

Going back under, my eyes fixed immediately on the brown line and I pictured myself flying above the vineyards, not the vineyards that I had been living on for the past eight months, but the vineyard of my childhood dreams, the vineyard I saw down the cooking corridor of my high school.

'I thought I would belong in a place where it was just me and the land.' I thought to myself, continuing to stare at the line. 'I thought I would belong.' 'I thought I would belong.'

I came up for air.

Straight back under I went, feeling like I had gone slightly deeper than before and I continued to swim staring straight down, almost forgetting where I really was. I felt extremely faint. Somewhere in the back of my mind my conscience was screaming at me to get out the pool, but my demons were far too prevalent in the forefront of my mind for me to hear, let alone listen.

'You don't grow tired of a place you belong.' My mind was telling me. 'Why did you think you did? Why did you think this was your home? This is not your home.' I noticed the brown line I was staring deeply into grow ever so slightly darker. 'This is not your home. You are kidding yourself.'

I started to feel like I needed air, but I stayed under. I was too deep in my thoughts to come up. Then, suddenly, I felt my hand smash into something hard and I realised I was at the end of the pool.

I dragged myself up against the side and breathed in deeply, feeling even more lightheaded, but it was satisfying to be able to breathe air.

Without even thinking, I pushed myself off the side again, so quickly I didn't even manage to push myself completely under the surface. I swam in breaststroke slowly along the surface which was exactly level with my goggles.

I could see above the surface and below the surface as the water flowed at the plastic of my goggles, which had let a very small bit of water into both sides.

'This is where you belong.' The voice in my head began again. I couldn't hear the voice; I could just feel it in my head, just like the pressure from the water around me. 'Nowhere. Look above the surface. Look below the surface. It's that mid ground you live in. It's that mid ground you will always live in. You don't belong above the surface or below the surface, just like you don't belong in London, or Belet. Nowhere. Just here. Nowhere. Nowhere.'

I tilted my head up for air and gulped a huge mouthful of water. I coughed and spluttered and leant forward to go back under and then back up so my eyes were level with the surface again so I could see both above and below.

'Go,' my mum's voice in my head said all of a sudden. 'Go.'

'Go where?' I thought, I might have even almost said. 'Go where?' 'Go where?' 'Go where?' 'I've tried to find my place, mum!' My thoughts were screaming, screaming at my demons; a huge war was raging in the very forefront of my head. Nothing else seemed to matter, absolutely nothing.

I needed air but I didn't care. I was beyond caring about things as petty as air, as petty as life and death. All that ran through my mind was disappointment; guilt that I had not become the contented, settled person my parents had hoped for me; anger at myself for not being able to belong, however much I tried.

'Go.' The voice said again, loud in my mind so that I swear I could actually physically hear it. My mum's voice was distorted, it sounded deep and angry as if it was ashamed of me, as if it didn't care anymore, as if it had given up and it was just telling me out of duty.

Then I did something I still to this day cannot explain. I have put it down to a nervous breakdown mixed with audible hallucinations from my ill state, but my lack of control at that moment still scares me.

I opened my mouth wide under the water and yelled as loudly as I could, 'Go where!' I heard nothing and immediately water filled my mouth and in shock I gasped for air. I felt water going straight down my windpipe and my lungs beginning to fill. I gasped again and more water filled my nose and mouth. An overwhelming dizziness came over me, my head felt unimaginably heavy but light and empty at the same time. I went to reach up to the surface as if I was going to try to pull myself up, but my arms just fell through the water, splashing, and bubbles of water everywhere around me. As I tried to rise up to the surface, I felt my body turning around and I felt as though I had no control at all of its actions. Frantically I kicked my arms and legs to try to get to the surface but I felt too heavy to rise, as if I was full of lead, as if something was dragging me down. I breathed in uncontrollably again, desperate,

desperate for air. All I could think about was air, nothing else. My windpipe was full of water, I was coughing and spluttering and every time I did, I breathed in again and every time I fell further towards the floor of the pool.

A feeling came over me that my demons had finally escaped the confines of my mind and had become physical beings hiding in the water with me. They were strangling me, suffocating me.

I knew I was drowning.

My desperate need for air, with every other feeling I had, began to fade into the deep dizziness inside me, the sheer tiredness. I had no energy to kick my legs or flap my arms; no energy to keep on trying. My brain felt soaked through, even my thoughts were escaping me. There was just a small part of my mind that seemed to still be working; the part that knew that what I was feeling, this slow descent into pitch darkness was the feeling of death.

I knew I was going to die.

Totally consumed by the dizziness that had surrounded me, I watched the surface way above me rise and rise away as I felt myself floating gracefully towards the floor.

My eyes were open as wide as they had ever been, vacant and still. Through the water and above the surface, which now felt miles and miles away, I could see a bright yellow light on the white of the ceiling shining straight through to me.

It shone like gold in the emptiness above me and I could stare right at it, my eyes fixed and unwavering.

I didn't have the need to blink; my eyes felt like they were fading away, as did every part of my body and my mind, all that was left was this golden light shining through the miles of water above me, the golden light, that shone straight into my dying mind like either the hope of a light at the end of the tunnel, or the hope of a sunrise on the horizon.

Sixteen

A bright light seeps through my eyelids and illuminates the darkness. I can't remember where I am or how long I have been there. All I can remember is an ongoing darkness; the feeling that I am aware of my existence but only just. I feel my eyes slowly open and all I can see is light, so I try to cover them with my hands. I feel weak and tired.

It floods in like water and I feel like I am floating in it, like the light that's filling the room around me is covering my entire body and drowning me.

I drift back into the black and become aware of the silence before losing my awareness all together.

The next thing I know there is a rattling near me and my eyes open much faster than before.

Again, the brightness is almost overwhelming so I have to blink quite a few times to ease into it. I feel like I have been in the dark for so long. Gradually the light starts to fade enough for me to make out the figures around me, the outline of the window, the chair in the corner and the person who had just woken me up.

'James.' There's a woman's voice coming from the direction of the person. It startles me and I flinch. 'Sorry,' said the woman, very softly.

Everything in the room is gradually becoming clearer as the almost unbearable brightness continues to fade away. I can see the window and through it, the view of a neatly trimmed garden and a light grey sky. However, even though the sky looks dull, there still seems to be an incredible brightness out there. I know why. Everything is covered in a thin layer of snow and more snowflakes are trickling gracefully down, making everything appear light and pure. I look at the chair in the corner and notice it's got an emerald green cushion on it with loads of holes in and a mahogany looking back. I also notice a vase in the corner with some flowers in. My eyes move slowly over to the woman and I see she is wearing all white, like a nurse.

"Where," I begin, but as I do I suddenly realise that my voice is hardly more than a whisper. "What's wrong with me?" I ask instead.

"Do you know where you are, James?" says the nurse.

"No. I can't remember anything," I reply weakly. "I'm in a hospital," I say, partly to myself.

"What's your name?" she says.

"James."

"And that's not because you heard me say it a minute ago?" she asks.

"No," I reply. "I know my name."

"What else do you know?" she says, "Tell me." She's standing just by the bed. My eyes wander from her to the bed sheets. They were all white and clean. I look vacantly around the room as I began to quietly speak.

"I'm twenty-six. I live in St John's Wood."

"St John's Wood?" asks the nurse, sounding surprised. I notice that she has an English accent. I feel surprised myself but I don't know why. "In London?"

"Yes," I confirm.

"James," she begins in her soft tone, "you're in France."

I give her an unconvincing look. 'France?' I think to myself, not believing it.

"You're in the Royal Bordeaux Hospital." She gives me a comforting smile. "Everything is okay. Are you ready to hear everything?"

"Yes," I reply, confusion engulfing my mind. I have no idea what I'm about to hear but I don't feel like anything would surprise me. As far as I know, I'm in some hospital in London because obviously something has happened that has damaged my memory. I don't know how long I have been here for but I must have had quite a while off work. I remember clearly how much I hate my job and how I feel like I don't belong. I know I have been thinking about packing everything in and going somewhere for a while now. The nurse begins to speak.

"You have been living in a place called Belet in Bordeaux for nine months. It says on your records that you use to live in St John's Wood, but you left in quite an impulsive fashion." She stopped talking to let me take it in, but I didn't need to, I accepted what she was saying but I didn't believe it. I didn't know if it was a mix up or some sort of sick joke, but I felt too weak to do anything other than lie there and let the whole thing play out. However, I did know that I had memory loss so I didn't really rule anything out. 'Bordeaux,' I thought; and my mind started to think back to my dreams of vineyards. She continues, cutting my imagination short, "You currently live with a gentleman named John Abraham. Does that ring any bells?"

I think for a second and then answer, "No." I wonder if it should and how this John person would feel about it.

"Don't worry about any of this, James. I want you to know that this is completely normal after waking up from a coma."

'A coma!' I think, and suddenly everything feels a bit more serious, a bit more worrying. I think the nurse saw this in my eyes.

"It's understood that two weeks ago, after a night out at a jazz club in Bordeaux, you decided to go for a swim in 'Pont Route Public Pool.' You were found to be heavily intoxicated." She pauses. "You almost drowned. The cameras show you were under water for nearly three minutes. Luckily the lifeguard managed to pull you out of the water and resuscitate you, but you became unconscious and so he called the ambulance. You began to come round slightly when the paramedics got to you, but on the way to the hospital you slipped into a coma."

I couldn't remember anything but something inside me had started to tell me that it was true. I felt a sick feeling coming over me as if my body was beginning to remember before my mind.

"How long have I been in a coma for?" I ask, my words only just coming out. I dread hearing the answer. 'What if I've been lying in this bed for years?' I shuddered at the thought. Then I thankfully remembered that she had said that I had been in France for nine months. I still couldn't remember.

"The incident happened two weeks ago. You didn't wake up for a week. For the past week you have been on and off, waking up and then drifting off again. We've spoken a couple of times. We haven't been unduly worried because you have shown good signs of progress. Every day you are awake for longer and seem more alert." She smiled.

185

"We've spoken before?" I ask, disturbed at the fact I couldn't remember.

"Yes James. I believe we spoke on Thursday, then on Saturday and then on Wednesday. This morning you were beginning to stir but you didn't say anything. You opened your eyes but you didn't notice me in the room and then you covered your eyes with your hands. It's quite common to be light sensitive when you come round, James."

I believe what the nurse is saying to me; after all it's all I know. I feel fresh and new as if I have woken up from a very long sleep. I suppose this is exactly what I have done but it was different to a normal sleep. It was dark and empty; a sleep full of nothingness and waking up from a long sleep, having had no dreams, is a strange, strange feeling.

I feel an itch on my chin so I scratch it. My arm feels heavy as I lift my hand to my face. A huge shock hits me when I feel a beard. It is both disturbing and reassuring that I am being told the truth.

"Speaking of which," the nurse begins and I remind myself what she is talking about, "would you like me to close the blinds. It is quite bright outside today because of the snow and it is important you get all the rest you can at this stage."

I tell her that I want her to shut the blinds. I am tired and want to go back to sleep but dread forgetting everything again. I hope my memory will come back to me soon, but I fear it wouldn't. It feels like I don't exist, like I am just a body lying here with no past.

I watch as the nurse turns away and walks over to the window. Outside, the falling snow is getting heavier, the flakes are getting thicker, and the glistening white layer on top of the garden is growing higher.

I want to be out there; to stand in the cold light of day and put my face to the sky, feeling the snowflakes drop onto my skin but I am too tired and too weak to move. I feel trapped by my own body. The window that stands between the garden and me is no more than a metaphor for the fact that I can't get to the other side. It isn't the glass standing in my way; it is myself. The whole thought process reminds me of something but I am not quite sure what. I remember that I have never felt like I have belonged but I can't remember anything specific other than the big traumatic events in my life.

The clutter of the blinds snaps me out of my deep thought as the nurse wriggles the cord around, trying to close the blinds. Then, all at once, they slip and fell to the windowsill. They hit it with a deep clunk and I know the noise, I feel the noise; the noise of a big lock turning in a heavy black door, the noise that makes me question where I have heard it before. I remember standing by the front door of the mansion, the vineyard behind me, rain falling heavily, a man standing by a waiting taxi, having heard the clunk and wondering where I have heard it before. I remember. It was the falling blind in my year nine history class, as I stared out of the window at the withered magnolia tree; the clunk of the blind hitting the windowsill, like the shutter to the vault I've stayed trapped inside my entire life.

Then, without saying anything; as the nurse quietly leaves the room, leaving the door ajar behind her, all the memories gradually begin to flood back into my mind, just like the water I had been drowning in two weeks earlier, just like the demons my mind have been drowning in most my life.

Quite suddenly, my tiredness leaves me and instead of drifting back off to sleep, I lay there remembering more and more with every second, until eventually, by the time the nurse comes back in later that day, I am still very much awake; and have remembered everything.

****

There's a big bang and I wake up suddenly. I had been dreaming the usual dream; lying hopelessly on the floor staring at the white walls that surrounded me, knowing deep down that there was no escape. I opened my eyes fast and wide when I woke.

It was John.

The room seemed bright even though I noticed that the blinds were still closed, however my eyes didn't feel as sensitive to the light and I felt slightly healthier and slightly stronger. I dreaded opening my mouth to talk because I didn't want to sound weak, as it would make me feel weak again. I wondered how long I had slept for this time. John walked over to the bed looking at me with half a smile.

"Fancy going for a swim, drunk," he said, sounding like he was half joking half being serious.

"How," I said, and I noticed my voice was quite a bit stronger and louder. I took a big swallow and continued. "How long have I been asleep for this time?"

"Not long this time," John replied. "You seem a lot brighter this time. Last time I visited, you could open your eyes but you just looked vacantly around the room not even realising I was here."

It felt horrible to think about that; it felt like it wasn't me.

John walked over to the blind and drew it up, revealing the window and the view of the garden. Snowflakes were falling heavily from the sky and the garden was covered in a thick layer of perfect white snow.

"The doctors say give it a few more days and you should be good to go," John said, turning away from the window to speak to me.

I was annoyed at John. I had seen a different side to him at the jazz club. I realised what he was like; the sort of person to take what he wants when he wants. He didn't seem like he gave much regard to anyone but himself. I still liked him as a friend very much, but I just knew where I stood with him. He wasn't family.

"I wondered where you'd got to, when I woke up the following morning back at the house," John told me, coming closer. "I thought you must have gone off with someone or something."

"No," I replied.

"Then I got the call," he continued without listening to me. "The hospital, they told me you were in a coma and that you had nearly drowned."

"Thank god for the lifeguard," I said, with little expression on my face.

"The lifeguard," John said, with a snigger. "That lifeguard is in deep shit. He'll be lucky if he isn't sentenced, James."

"Why?"

"Why?" John repeated. "Don't you remember?"

"What?"

"You were under water for nearly three minutes. They say he didn't even notice until you had been under for two. It's disgusting. He deserves to go down."

I was in two minds, remembering the lifeguard falling asleep on the chair. He had saved my life, but also could have saved me from being in a coma if he was doing his job properly.

"I remember," I said to John.

"He was half asleep when he should have been watching you. You were the only one in the pool. Who is allowed to nearly drown when they are the only one in the pool?" John seemed genuinely annoyed and it made me feel like he may have cared a bit more than I had previously thought. "Anyway," he continued, "I need to get back, I've got somebody coming round for a meeting."

"A meeting?" I asked.

"Don't worry about it. Get some rest. Let me take care of the vineyard for now." John put his hand on my shoulder and patted it once, slowing down his pace. "Right!" he said suddenly and walked over to the door. "See you soon."

I hadn't been at the vineyard for over two weeks. Was I really as essential as I thought I was? I started to think about the vines growing steadily without me there. I thought I should say something to take my mind off it.

"Where are my flowers?" I joked as John opened the door.

"They're there," he replied, pointing to the vase in the corner, "in the corner."

"Oh," I replied, remembering seeing them in one of my waking bouts. "You got them?" I said, almost laughing, but with little energy or air.

"Yes," said John smiling in a single outward breath. "Okay, must go."

"Bye John," I said, and he walked out the door, leaving it ajar behind him.

I listened to his footsteps as he walked quickly away and as the tapping of his shoes on the wooden floor faded into the distance, I couldn't help but feel that he was hiding something from me.

****

When I was finally let out, I had been in hospital for just over three weeks.

John was standing at my door in a black leather jacket, his black and grey hair neatly trimmed and shining in the artificial hospital light.

The snow outside had melted and the ground was now dry. Outside the window, the garden looked still and cold under the crisp November air.

As we walked along the corridor to the exit, I spoke to John.

"I've been looking on the hospital computers and apparently the trains don't take us all the way. We'll have to take a taxi from the nearest station back to Belet, or maybe there will be a bus. How do you usually get back?" I asked.

John looked at me and smiled slyly. "I don't know the bus route," he replied.

"How do you usually get back then?" I repeated my question.

We were approaching the automatic revolving doors to the car park.

"Well," he began, just before we walked through the doors in separate sections, "I thought I would buy you a recovery present."

I understood what he meant as he put his hand in his trouser pocket almost as if it was scripted; right on cue, he pulled out an electric key and looked at me. Then without either of us saying anything as we continued to walk into the car park, he pointed his key at a car.

It wasn't just any old car; it was a Daimler Super Eight. Its golden lights flashed twice as he pressed the button on the key and he looked at me again, grinning widely.

"You bought a Daimler?" I said in shock.

"I sure did, James, for you."

"And I'm guessing you took the money out of the business account?" I asked, stopping walking.

John stopped as well.

"Well," he began, "who says we can't treat ourselves once in a while." He looked over to the car, looking like he was signalling me to do the same. "Not many were made you know."

"How much did you take out to buy it?" I asked, without even glancing back at the car. We were not supposed to spend any of the money from the business account. We paid ourselves a very generous salary from the account and we were supposed to only spend money out of that. But I knew how expensive this car was and even with John's salary of just over a hundred thousand a year, he wouldn't have been able to afford this in only a few months.

"Well I'm sure you know James, they only sell cars like this at auction don't they." He hadn't taken his eyes off the car.

"How much?" I asked again.

"It was just under two hundred, okay?" John snapped. Then he continued as if in fear that if he didn't, I would. "I thought you might be a little bit more grateful if I'm honest with you."

"Grateful?" I said with almost a shout. I couldn't believe what I was hearing. "You go out and buy 'me' a Daimler, which I'm guessing you're obviously insured on as well, with our business account and expect me to be grateful?"

"'My' business account," John replied with a calm, but raised voice.

"What?"

"That's 'my' business account."

Then I regrettably remembered that I had signed ownership of the vineyard over to him; that meant the account as well and everything in it.

I was speechless for a few moments.

"Okay, John," I replied quietly, defeated.

'Was this what he was hiding?' I thought to myself, convinced for some reason unbeknown to me that there was something else as well. 'Was the car meant to be a peace offering for this other thing, a peace offering that backfired?'

No one had said anything for a minute, we were just both standing there, in the car park.

"And are you going to tell me what else there is you're hiding?" I said, sounding sure of myself.

John suddenly looked at me and snapped, 'nothing,' before walking over to the car.

I stood there and watched as he opened the door and carefully got in as if it was a rare antique he was trying not to scratch. I thought about getting the train back but I still felt quite weak and I knew it wouldn't be a wise idea, so I begrudgingly walked over to the car.

It was dark green with a golden strip running its length. It glistened in the afternoon sun, looking like it had just been cleaned.

I noticed John smile slightly as I went to open the door, as if he thought he had won.

The door was solid and I got in and sat down on something similar to an armchair and closed the door. It thudded shut.

"Quite something, isn't it?" John said, and I could see him looking at me out of the corner of my eye, with a look of accomplishment in his eyes.

"Well," I replied, hating myself even before I said it, "I'm not going to lie."

I smiled, partly because I wanted to keep the peace, but partly because as I rested back on the cloth of the chair that seemed to melt itself around my back, I couldn't help it.

John said nothing and put his foot on the accelerator. I felt myself fall slightly back into the chair. It was as comfortable as a new mattress and it was extremely difficult to stay annoyed.

But something that wasn't difficult was the decision my mind was subconsciously making as I watched the hospital car park roll smoothly away and we drove back to a place I had only recently realised had never been my home.

Seventeen

It was dark and even in my winter coat I could feel the chill coming through like an arctic breeze. It was so quiet, so empty; nothing other than the whistling of the wind through the vines that hid under the early morning darkness.

I'd seen the grape bushes when I had arrived back with John in the Daimler last night. We'd rolled up the dusty track and parked just outside the big black door of the mansion. Sitting there, on the rocking chair by the shed, I remembered how the grape bushes had grown so well in my absence, as if even the land was telling me that I wasn't needed at all.

I wondered if any vines had been infected and if that infection would have spread to other vines and damaged any, if in my absence anything had been left and not maintained; I hoped it had but I knew as I looked out the night before that even if it had, it was only minor.

I dreaded the sun rising because I knew that when it did, I would look out onto the vineyard and feel like I didn't belong.

The worst part was I didn't even really know why. There was just something inside me telling me that I never did; that even when I thought I had done, I was just kidding myself.

A huge gust of wind blew in from the darkness of the land that spread out into the distance. I felt its vastness carried in the wind as it hit and stung my face.

At least in London, I was distracted from the never ending thoughts that played over and over in my head; the voice of my past that told me repeatedly that no matter how hard I tried, I would never belong. The demons would scream at me on the train every day on my way to work but then when I got to work I would be too busy meeting clients and dealing with numbers to pay any attention to them.

Here in Belet, I knew that now the demons had sneaked back into my head, there would be nothing to distract me from the poison that leaked out of them and seeped into my head. They would play over and over and over until – until I couldn't take it anymore.

I remembered how Eric couldn't even cope in London, even with all the distractions of the city. I had so much faith that I would fare better here in Belet; I suppose I needed that faith to get by for as long as I did, but now that faith was gone.

I prayed that when I saw the sun come up and watched as its golden rays sprinkled onto the land, that I would feel different; that I would somehow be reminded that I did belong, in my heart I knew the truth, the truth that after all these years, I had only just realised, that it wasn't the bullying or the loneliness, it wasn't my career or my country, it wasn't my life that made me feel as though I didn't belong; it was me.

The feeling was inside me and I didn't know why. But I finally knew the truth; that there was no point coming to Belet; that however far I walk into the horizon, I will never be truly free.

There was another huge gust of wind, even stronger than the last; and as it hits my face, I heard a smashing sound and all of a sudden the small yellow light that hung from the top of the shed goes out and I am left in the darkness.

And there I am, alone, in the cold, in the dark, knowing that I don't belong and dreading, *dreading,* the sunrise.

****

I hear a loud knocking at the door from the library. It felt like it woke me up but I don't think I had been asleep; maybe I had drifted off without realising.

I had spent most the day in the library, trying to stay out of John's way to avoid getting into any arguments.

John wasn't exactly a hard person to read but it was difficult to tell if he knew something was up with me. I think he was so caught up in his own secrets that he paid little attention to the obvious worry I had written all over my face. I knew it was going to come as a surprise to him when I told him that I was leaving.

I'd been re-reading books I had already read, trying to distract my mind from reality by getting lost in fiction, but I couldn't really get into anything. It took me back to my school days where I would spend all lunch reading on my own, trying not to look pitiful and trying to take my mind off my demons that I didn't know would eventually ruin my life. Most of the day was spent with the book open on my lap with me thinking back to my school days and my life, more than the words I was vacantly reading.

As I walked out of the room, I felt my legs aching as I had been sitting down for far too long and I could hear that John had already answered the door.

197

I hobbled down the narrow corridor and through the doors to the hallway and just as I walked through the final door, I heard the front door clunk shut.

John is standing there next to an old man, wavy grey hair hanging down to his shoulders under a brown flat cap. Even under his long light brown overcoat, I can see he is thin and frail looking. His face is that of a skull wrapped in a thin layer of creased skin. He looks like a withered memory of a well-chiselled man. But the strange part was that even with all that, he still gave the impression of looking rather fit and healthy; well looked after and well groomed.

He caught my eye the second I stumbled tiredly into the room and walked over effortlessly.

"You must be James," he smiled, creasing his cheeks up even more and showing straight but browning teeth. His hand reached out to shake mine, so I did.

"And you are?" I asked with a straight face.

"My name is Manrico," he replied proudly, straightening up his body. His voice was harsh and croaky with only a slight French accent. "I'm head of the French Wine Association."

"Manrico?" I said. "I've read your letter." 'What was he doing here?' "What brings you to Belet?"

Both Manrico and John's faces turned serious; Manrico looking at me, John looking at the floor. Then Manrico turned to John.

"I thought you would have told him," he said.

John didn't reply and continued to look down.

Manrico's face looked annoyed and disappointed. He let out a huge sigh. "John," he said to himself angrily.

John looked up and jumped back to life. "Let's go inside," he said invitingly and then looked over at me. "James, I'll explain everything."

John turned and walked through the doors into the lounge and Manrico followed on behind, glancing over at me as if to apologise as he did. I followed behind, feeling like I was having a guided tour of some unknown house.

We each took a chair in the lounge.

I looked at John.

"Tell James," Manrico commanded calmly.

John swallowed and braced himself. Then after a few moments, he began.

"James, now let me talk before you, before you," he couldn't get his word out. "Just listen, okay?"

"I'm listening," I replied coldly.

"Okay. About two weeks ago somebody came to the door. His name was David Wheeler. He was English. He said he was from a company called Bone and Wheeler fund management." I didn't recognise the name and I knew most of the fund management companies in London, but I continued to listen intently. "I was made an offer for the vineyard, James."

I think my mouth opened in shock. I was waiting for him to say that, but when he did, I still couldn't help it. I didn't say anything; I just looked over at Manrico, who had dropped his head to the floor.

There was silence for a while. Everybody was waiting for somebody else to talk.

"That is why I am here today, James," Manrico said, raising his head. He had a disappointed look in his eyes and he said the next few words as if he was gritting his teeth, "To organise the deal."

"I've been thinking for a few months now about the idea," John began again. "I'm going to be honest with you; I see no reason to lie now. Yes, at first it felt good being here, but after the initial excitement, I soon realised that I'm not cut out to run a place like this. I'm not the sort of person that settles in one place for the rest of my life, and I saw my future if I was to stay here. I'm too used to moving around."

I didn't want to hear it. His voice sounded like nothing but pure betrayal.

"He offered us forty-five million." I noticed him try to hide his sick smile. "That's obviously twenty for the money in the business account and twenty-five for the house, the land and…" he paused.

My ears pricked up again at the sudden silence. I had been trying to block out the terrible noise coming from his mouth, but I was curious about what he was about to say.

"And?" Manrico said, telling John to tell me.

John said nothing for a few moments and then said it so quietly and shamefully, I could just about hear him, "And the name."

I got up and walked straight over to the door, not even making eye contact with John as I did so.

"That's forty-five million Euros in our account, James!" John said loudly as I reached the door.

"'Your' account," I replied, opening the door calmly so as to be the bigger man, but furious inside. I walked out the room, my blood boiling and without looking back I said, half to myself, but so that John could hear, 'You've made that perfectly clear.'

****

200

I must have been outside for a good few hours, just strolling through the vineyard.

I wasn't upset. The vineyard had begun to feel like nothing to me, just a mere blip in the life I didn't belong in. I was just angry at how John had gone behind my back, having seen first-hand how much work I had put into the place over the harvest, and taken the liberty of the biggest decision one can make in business. I had had the decency to sign the entire place over to him and this is how he had repaid me. Even though I now cared little about Bernard's legacy, I did care about the future of the place I had dedicated a portion of my life to, and I cared just as much about the principle of it; the history of the place and how John had taken it into his own hands to throw it all away. He hadn't only betrayed me, but he had betrayed his own ancestors. He had single-handedly put an end to over three hundred years of tradition.

Even though it was getting on for sunset and ice cold outside, the sun was shining brightly down and I was looking at the ground, squinting as I walked. I was quite near to the house and I could see the shed in the distance to the right. I could even see the wooden decking next to it, the light still lying smashed on the wood.

I heard footsteps and could see a shadow approaching me. I looked up and saw Manrico walking briskly towards me. From a distance he would look like a young man, walking with ease. When he neared me, he pulled his cap down to cover his eyes against the strong sunlight. His grey hair was glistening in the sun.

"James," he said, stopping in front of me, blocking my path. I had no choice but to stop as well.

"Manrico," I replied, nodding my head.

"Let us walk together for a while," Manrico said peacefully, and he turned and started to stroll. He somehow knew I hadn't moved, even though he hadn't looked back so he beckoned me along. "Come, James," he said.

I followed him along the pathways for a few minutes without either of us saying anything. I felt as though he was waiting for me to talk, but then he stopped by one of the grape bushes and leaned over, feeling the stalk and the leaves underneath.

"This is a very healthy vine," he said in his husky voice, smiling up at me and squinting in the strong late evening sun. He rose up and continued to stroll slowly along. "You have looked after them extraordinarily well, James."

"Thank you," I replied, looking at him from behind as we walked.

"You know I've been in the wine business for seventy years," he said. I said nothing; just continued to follow him.

"I know even in the short time you have been here you have done a great deal." He didn't turn back to talk, he just continued walking and looking ahead, as we walked along a path that lead away from the mansion and out into the vastness of the land. "Bernard would be proud."

I said nothing. I felt a shudder come over me at the mention of his name.

Manrico noticed my silence and turned around to look at me, without stopping walking. Then without saying anything, he turned back to face ahead again.

"I should have never sent that letter, James." I saw his head tilt back slightly and knew he was looking out deeply into the distance. "I should have never brought John here."

The sky was beginning to turn a darker shade of gloomy blue, and the chill was getting stronger and colder.

Manrico stopped and I stopped as well. It seemed like he had waited to say whatever he was about to say until we had reached this point, far away from the house, far away from John. "I say this with a heavy heart," he began, looking right at me, "but you were the son Bernard should have had."

I was looking at him, but when I heard Bernard's name, my eyebrows lowered and I looked at the ground, which now appeared quite dark in the setting sun.

"Why must you be so silent, James? Why do you fall especially silent when I say his name?"

I looked up at him, trying to work out if he knew the truth or not. I had presumed he didn't know what had happened because of the letter, but I couldn't help but feel as if Manrico was the sort of man who would know everything about everything and everyone. 'Maybe,' I thought, 'he hadn't told anyone about Bernard because of the damage it would do to the name and the industry.' I suddenly thought I had nothing to lose, so I decided to just ask him straight.

"Don't you know about Bernard, Manrico?"

"Know what?" he asked, his eyebrows raised.

"I think you know what," I replied.

Marico's face looked puzzled. I began to think he didn't.

"That he killed his wife and child?" I asked, beginning to doubt my words.

"What?" Manrico's face turned sour.

I looked at him, confused as to which one of us was being left in the dark.

"Bernard did not kill his wife and child, James," Manrico said, obviously extremely annoyed at me for disrespecting somebody who I suddenly realised must have been a dear old friend.

"But, but," I stuttered.

"Why would you think that?" he asked me, concerned, his voice croakier than ever.

"I," I began, "well, what happened to them then?"

Manrico looked at me with stern eyes, locked intently on mine. "Julia and Ben, may god rest their souls, they drowned in the terrible September flood of eighty-nine." I could see the honesty and sorrow in his old eyes.

A huge wave of guilt came over me.

Manrico continued. "Bernard did all he could to save them, but you know these hills, James; the currents were just far too strong." He stopped and looked like he wasn't able to continue with the story, but he did. "When Bernard finally managed to pull them out of the water; they were cold and lifeless. It was a terrible, terrible time for everyone. I can only imagine what agony he must have felt. I accompanied Bernard to the morgue. I remember it like it was yesterday; the radio was on in the reception, Bernard stood there having not even changed since the incident, even though it had been two days. He was shaking like a leaf. The radio was hazy but we heard the presenter say," Manrico coughed loudly and quickly pulled out a tissue from his pocket and held it to his mouth. Then he continued. "We heard the presenter say that two days ago the heavens had opened. Bernard said to me in a voice so shaky, he sounded like he was speaking from beyond the grave, he said, 'it wasn't heaven that had opened; it was hell.' We then went into the morgue and that was the last thing he said for many years. He fell out of touch with all of his friends and with all his acquaintances in the wine business and became a recluse here in his Chateau. He lived a solitary life for twenty-five years before you turned up. It didn't help that he was quite a solitary man anyway, as you very well know, that is why Julia left for London in the first place."

There were tears trickling down my cheeks. I couldn't believe it. I felt absolutely terrible for judging such a good man, a man who had experienced so much pain in his life.

"Why didn't you come to his funeral?" I asked.

"I didn't know, James. I'd lost contact with Bernard, how would I have known? Bernard had written to me years earlier saying he didn't want to hear from me or anyone anymore; that he just wanted to be left on his own. I only knew him from then on through a business sense, and I only found out he was ill, when there was a leak from the hospital records in the wine news. I knew Bernard would still be here anyway, he would never leave this place, it was so much more than just a vineyard to him; it was his heritage." Manrico smiled a bit at Bernard's memory. "But I have visited his grave many times when I found out where he had been buried."

More tears rolled down my face when I thought about the fact that I hadn't visited his grave once. After all, I had convinced myself that he was a murderer. I could see him looking down at me, feeling betrayed by me as much as the son he never knew he had who waited back at the mansion.

"It's not your fault, you didn't know, James," Manrico said comfortingly walking over and putting his hand on my shoulder. "Come on," he said, taking his hand off and starting to walk back down the path we had earlier come down. "It's getting dark, we best get back."

I followed on, looking up at the sky, realising how dark it now was. I was so captivated by Manrico's story and caught up in my guilt and sorrow that I hadn't even noticed the sun set. Now, as we walked, all that was left to light the path ahead was the leftover light after the sunset faded away into the unhopeful evening land.

"Does John know?" I asked, the moment the question popped into my head, the lights from the few windows in the mansion drawing nearer in the dark.

Even though I had wanted to leave John with a good image of his late father, I thought it was the right thing to do to tell him what I believed to be the truth; something I thought I never had been given. That's why I had told John about the gravestones in the woods and he had agreed that their blood must have been on Bernard's hands.

I was desperate to know if John knew the truth about Bernard's innocence and had still decided to go ahead with selling his father's legacy. What John was doing was unforgiving enough, even with the idea that Bernard was a murderer. If John knew that his father was innocent and was still going ahead with selling his estate and his name then that, in my opinion, would be no less than a disgrace.

"John didn't first contact me to deal with the sale, James," Manrico began.

The path had widened enough for us to walk next to each other and Manrico looked back and forth from me to the dark path as he spoke.

"No, John first contacted me nearly two months ago to find out more about his family." Manrico looked so full of pent up grief and anger, his words so full of woe. "He has known since then, James."

"Why wouldn't he tell me?" I asked in horror.

"You know why, don't you?" Manrico said in disgust.

I thought for a while and then replied, half asking if I was correct in what I thought, "Because as long as I saw

Bernard as a murderer, I wouldn't disagree too much with the sale?"

Manrico looked at me with a straight and serious face, "Precisely," he croaked.

And we continued towards the mansion, both of us having nothing more to say, one foot at a time, being careful not to trip in the now almost pitch dark, Manrico having turned into no more than a black figure moving swiftly through the vines in front of me.

Eighteen

The days that followed saw me organising my flights back to London. I had booked a British Airways flight from Bordeaux Merignac Airport to Heathrow. It was in two days' time.

I thought about what I was going to do back in London, where I was going to work, and where I was going to live. I knew that I was going to feel as though I didn't belong but I also knew that I would have no choice but to accept it.

In searching for a place I would belong, I discovered that I never would. I suppose at least in that sense, the last nine months had been a success.

I didn't mention anything to John; in fact, I had hardly even spoken to John since the visit from Manrico. Anyway, John was too busy organising the sale of the place to notice me mooching solemnly around the house.

All the closeness I had ever felt for John had vanished and it made me realise how little I really did feel about him when I thought about how quickly I had been able to forget that we had ever been friends.

I walked a couple of times along the pathways of the vineyard seeing if my demons would let me feel anything, any peace or belonging but as I expected, they didn't; all I felt was hostility.

Yes, I felt the wind and the rain and the sun and I heard the whistling of the breeze and the birds chirping but none of it meant anything more than what it was. The birds would sing and that is all I would hear – birdsong. My mind made me feel no longer welcome.

All I wanted to do was start heading back to London. It's not that I saw London as home; it's just that I wanted this chapter of my life to be over and my next one to begin. I knew I would feel the same in London; I knew I would feel like this for the rest of my life but I also knew that there was nothing I could do about it, and at least in London I would have the distraction of the city keeping my demons at bay.

There was just one last thing I had to do before I left.

****

John was surprised when I told him what I was doing. He said that he didn't see it coming but I didn't know whether to believe him or not. He said that despite our differences and our disagreements, he would miss me and he wanted me to stay in touch. I lied and told him likewise. I asked him what he was going to do after the sale had gone through and he told me that he was going to live his life. He asked me what *I* was going to do and I answered the same, but one didn't have to know me to have been able to hear the doubt in my voice.

I walked to the door with my bags and out onto the doorstep, closing it behind me. It looked as black and heavy as the first day I'd seen it. I remembered Bernard saying; 'Not even Vesuvius would wake me up," and I smiled at the fond memory; at the time I felt like I belonged here.

I walked down the dusty track just as my taxi pulled in through the gates past the shed. The golden strip along the side of the Daimler glistened in the light and caught my eye as I walked past it.

When my taxi pulled over, I put my bags on the back seat and got in the front.

"Going to the airport?" the driver asked in a thick French accent.

"Yes," I replied, looking out of the window back at the mansion. "But I want to stop on the way for about twenty minutes; I'll pay you for your time."

"Where?" asked the taxi driver.

"La Chartreuse," I replied, still looking back at the mansion.

"The cemetery?"

"Yes," I replied.

"Okay," said the taxi driver and we started to drive away, sand lifting up behind the car.

I watched as the mansion drifted out of sight and we rolled past the shed. The rocking chair looked so still and empty as if no one had ever sat on it. I turned round to see the vineyard that stretched out through the back right window as far as the eye could see. It looked like a picture, a beautiful, beautiful picture; but no more than just that; the sort of place I wished I could call home. Then the bushes near the entrance gate obstructed my view, I turned back and looked out of the window just in time to see the old wooden signpost pass by. I knew that on the other side it said; 'Château Belet,' but from my side all I could see was plain wood, with nothing written on it at all.

We pulled out through the open gate and onto the old country lane that remained isolated from the world for miles and miles until it eventually lead into town. For a while I couldn't get the plain signpost out of my mind; it looked as empty as my heart felt as we drove further and further away from, not just a place I had called home for so long, but the place that had given me my final hope of belonging.

But eventually my mind was taken off the signpost because, even though I didn't care at all about appearing rude, the taxi driver had begun to strike up conversation with me. Everything he asked I answered quickly and without thought. He obviously knew that my mind was somewhere else.

****

So there I was, standing by Bernard's grave for the first time since I had buried him. The taxi driver was waiting for me out of sight and had said that even though he was busy he would give me half an hour. I looked at his name engraved on the stone. My eyes were dry but my heart was in tears.

"I'm sorry Bernard." I said out loud. There was nobody else around. A tear had begun to roll down my cheek. "I'm sorry for everything." "I'm sorry I thought it was you." I was in tears. I didn't wipe them away; it felt satisfying letting them fall down my face and onto the grass. "I'm sorry I let John do what he has done. I'm sorry what happened to you, for all the pain you had to suffer in your life. But mostly..." I stopped because I had to wipe my face, my nose was dripping over my top lip and into my mouth and my face was soaking wet. I could taste salt. I was sobbing and it was difficult to breath. "Mostly..." I had to stop again to take in air. "Mostly, I'm sorry I couldn't stay. I'm sorry I couldn't even give all your trying meaning in saving my life."

It was just Bernard's grave and me, nothing else was around. The graveyard was an empty void around us. I had never spoken such truths in all my life.

"Thank you for giving me the opportunity to belong. Thank you for giving my life the meaning I have always strived for. Thank you for being like a father to me." My tears had dried up, my shoes were wet. I put my hand on the gravestone. "Goodbye, Bernard," I said and I closed my eyes so that I would really feel him there, feel him looking down on me, hoping he would forgive me. "Goodbye."

I stayed there with my hand on the grave and my eyes closed for a few minutes before opening them and starting to walk back along the neatly trimmed grass pathway to the taxi.

My demons were silent for that time. It was almost as if they were giving me just a little bit of time to feel peace. I thought about staying here in the cemetery forever, just like the opening in the cemetery where Eric had been buried.

Would my life really be made up of empty chapters, always waiting for the next brief moment where my demons would subside enough for me to hear the silence.

Then, as I neared the small white gate I had come through and saw the taxi waiting for me, a thought came over me. It didn't feel as though it was my demons speaking to me; it felt different. It felt as though it was actually me speaking to myself for once, not the voices in my head speaking to me. It wasn't a thought of guilt or fear; it was a thought of acceptance.

'I'll never belong.'

Then I walked out of the gate and got into the front seat of the taxi.

"The airport?" asked the taxi driver with an empathetic look on his face as if he understood, I thought, even a fraction of what was going on in my head.

"Yes," I replied, "take me to the airport;"

And he drove off briskly, his empathy being overridden by his lack of time.

I didn't blame him. 'Everybody has a schedule,' I thought to myself. "Something to rush home for;"

And my heart sank.

Nineteen

I had been living back in England for ten years when I saw the article in the Evening Standard on the way home from the office.

I lived in Amersham, the final stop on the Metropolitan line, far out enough to feel like the countryside, but still connected to the city. I lived in a lovely detached house with my wife, Alice; and my two young children, Robert and Jane. Every day I would walk to the station with my briefcase and board the train. It took about an hour and a half to get to Canary Wharf, where I worked for a private equity firm, dealing with wealth management for a long list of very rich clients.

The trains seemed to grow more crammed every year, or maybe it was just me growing more and more claustrophobic. No, I'm pretty sure I was actually growing use to the busyness. It didn't bother me like it used to, after all, I had a young family to support, I had to lump it, I couldn't just up and go even if it did all get too much.

I read the article in the newspaper intently, without even noticing the stops going past.

'Château Belet, a historic mansion house in Bordeaux dating back to the sixteenth century burns to the ground in a huge blaze.

Thankfully, nobody was injured because the house has been vacant for the past four years after many attempts by various wine and investment management companies to bring it back to life.

It is said that after being sold to 'Bone and Wheeler' it started to go downhill, due to the fact that it had lost its heritage, something that is vital in the wine business.

Wine icon, Bernard Abraham, who ran the vineyard for over fifty years after taking it over from his own father, passed the estate down to his dear son, John Abraham, before he died. John ran the vineyard successfully and gave the world Belet's greatest harvest ever, before passing the vineyard on to 'Bone and Wheeler' as he believed the company needed 'new direction.'

Unfortunately, the move did not go well for the company and within a year it had fallen by half its value. The next harvest was the worst on record and investors soon began to latch on to the idea that it was a company on its way down.

After going through five different owners, the vineyard was finally put into administration six years after its sale and the estate was left deserted.

It is believed the fire started from a lightning strike and it didn't take long for the fire to spread, due to the fact that the property was largely made of wood, until the entire place was ablaze.

It is believed that even though the land has been left unmaintained for four years, it is able to be developed into either farmland for grazing cattle, or possibly for crops.

The late Manrico Marcellus, who was head of the French Wine Association for over fifty years is said to have been in tears at the press conference after Belet went in to administration.

It is a sad end to a beautiful story, but sometimes the most beautiful stories are just that, because of the ending sadness.'

When I finished reading the article, I realised that my hands were stiff and sweaty and the newspaper was scrunched up in my hands.

I looked up as the train doors closed at Chalfont and Latimer; my stop was next.

****

I had decided to never tell Alice about Belet. I wanted to when I first met her, but I didn't want her to know about the ghosts that haunted me. I wanted to try to have a fresh start when I met her – a new beginning. Of course I knew that they would still be there, waiting in the back of my mind for the rest of my days; sometimes they would be less prevalent than others, but they would never completely fade. I thought that if I push them far enough in then it might make it more difficult for them to come out, it might make their voice quieter, it might make it easier for me to get on with my life but I was wrong.

The more I tried to hide them from myself and pretend to myself that I was fine, the more prevalent they became. All I could do was leave them at the forefront of my mind and get on with my life, trying to ignore them.

Not a day went by when I didn't constantly remind myself that I didn't belong, that however far I walked into the horizon, I would never be truly free. Not a day went by where I didn't pray for peace, for silence, but I knew the day would never come.

I grew deeply depressed inside, but kept that hidden from my wife and children as well. It sometimes felt like I was falling down a deep hole that I had dug for myself, but the more years that went by, the more I knew I could never tell my wife. It felt as if I had had an affair or betrayed them all in some way; I think it's because in some way I had. I had never been the man I had pretended to be. Is that not betrayal at its finest?

One day I was out for a walk with them, Alice pushing Jane in her pram and Robert holding my hand. We were walking along a pathway through the fields that stretched all around Amersham and into the Chilterns.

Alice looked over at me in the sun and smiled lovingly. Her smile always reminded me of how my mum used to smile, with her eyes, as if she was looking right in to my soul. The only difference was my mum knew me. Alice never really had done, even though I know she thought she did.

She loved the man I wanted to be; the city worker, the content husband and father. To her, that was all there was to know and it was good to know that she thought she knew me. It made me feel like everything was almost true.

She asked me how my head was feeling and for a second I was unsure what she meant. Then I remembered that I had told her that I was seeing the doctor about an ongoing headache when I was really seeing the psychiatrist to discuss my depression and to be issued with some new pills.

I didn't even talk about the root of my depression to the psychiatrist, or any other of the twelve psychiatrists I had seen in the last eight years. I didn't see the point; I knew they wouldn't be able to help, I knew if I couldn't silence my demons then neither could they. I saw the psychiatrists as no more than a way to get free pills to calm me down, nothing else.

I looked at my wife as lovingly as I could. I did love her, I did love our two beautiful children, but sometimes when my mind was at its darkest point, something I had no control over at all, it was hard to feel any other emotion through the overpowering voices drowning my soul.

"It's much better honey," I began, smiling widely in the sun, "but I'm seeing the doctor in two weeks about a small cyst on my ear; it's nothing to worry about;"

And as we continued to walk along the grassy pathway, my family talking to each other about cartoons and school, I couldn't help but lose concentration as their voices seemed to drift away with the breeze and my awareness turned to the tall conifer trees that lined either side of the field.

Twenty

Even though I remember parts of Belet like it was yesterday, as a whole, it feels like a lifetime ago.

I remember when I first met Bernard; and I remember when I watched him slip away. I remember the first time I came across the woods at the edge of the vineyard and I remember when I returned to them and saw the gravestones. I remember when I first stumbled up the path, in the middle of the night and slept outside on the rocking chair by the shed, how at peace I was, how I felt such belonging. But most of all I remember the first time the idea that I still didn't belong crept back into the dark crevasses of my mind, and how that feeling grew and grew until I had no choice but to accept the truth.

The truth was that not only did I not belong in Belet, but that I didn't belong anywhere and never would. In the past, however bad life had got, however big my demons grew, I always had the final hope in the back of my mind that if it all got too much, I could run away. If Belet did anything for me, it made me realise that even this final hope wasn't possible. In discovering a place I thought would let me finally belong, I found out that I never could, because the thing I had always been trying to escape from, throughout school and work and life had been the one thing I never can.

I've lost count of the number of times I've had that recurring nightmare in recent years; the one with the endless network of identical white rooms linked by identical doors. I remember the first time I dreamt it. It was the night before I left for France. I should have seen it as a sign of things to come. My subconscious seemed to know how things would end up all along; it was just waiting for my conscious to catch up with it. It took almost a year.

****

Here I am, sitting on this packed Jubilee line train, on my way to Canary Wharf. Somebody just offered me their seat; I must look old. I must *feel* old as well because I accepted his offer and sat down. I suppose, I *am* old; I'm going to be sixty next month.

The other day my young grandson asked me how long I had been working in a tower for. He was fascinated with the idea of being so high up, in a literal sense. I told him many, many years. He then asked me if I enjoyed it and I couldn't lie to him like I do to everybody else, I couldn't exploit his innocence, so I told him I don't mind it, which, I guess, in some way is true. After a minute of what looked like deep thought, he asked me one more question, 'Why do you do it then, grandpa?' I pretended not to hear.

The train is rocking madly as we approach Green Park. The roaring noise as it hurtles along the tracks drowns out the noise of the demons that still pound almost constantly now in the back of my head. 'You can never escape. You can never escape. You can never escape.' On and on they go, as does the train.

We stop at Green Park.

I watch as quite a number of people get off and on, everybody's attention fixed completely on something or other, from newspapers to phones to crosswords.

I close my eyes to try to think about something to take my mind off the claustrophobia, which I have grown worryingly used to, but which is still unpleasant. I have never been comfortable passing Waterloo; it brings back too many memories.

The second I close my eyes, I'm in the white room, looking at the wall; no doors, just white. I force myself to picture something else, something happy and free. I picture my wife, her face there, right in front of mine, but her face as it was when I met her, not the aged, worn face I see now, which I still love just as much. Her youthful face in my mind's eye; she's beautiful, her blue eyes are like the open ocean or the everlasting sky. I'm lost in them, as if I've fallen into them and can't find my way back out. I have a horrible feeling inside me, a feeling that I have never deserved her, that I have always stopped her from doing better, that I've held her back in life. In my mind she tells me she loves me, but I can't stop apologising, 'I'm sorry, I'm sorry.' I keep saying to her, I'm begging her with everything I have to forgive me, she says that there is 'nothing to forgive,' but in my mind I feel like she too believes that there is and that she can't, so she kids herself that I haven't done her wrong in life, that I haven't held her back, with my depression, with my nightmares, with my lack of belonging.

Then, still begging her to forgive me, her face fades away into nothingness and somebody else appears. It's a man, he's huge, a body like an ape – it's Antosh, well at least, it's the idea of Antosh. I can't remember for the life of me what he looks like and I wouldn't want to, but here is

221

this man, towering above me even though in reality I am the same height as I remember him being. 'Oi! You little weed!' He's shouting and nudging me with clenched fists. Every time he does I go flying as if I'm made of air and my actual body flinches, but for some reason I have suddenly become obsessed with the idea of keeping my eyes closed.

I become aware that I am in a corridor, the cooking corridor. I look down at the tiled floor and imagine the lines of the tiles are pathways cutting through grape bush lined fields. I picture myself walking down them and even then, even with the sun beaming down, the fresh breeze on my face and the beautiful view of an everlasting horizon, I still feel trapped. There's a tear in my eye and I have to hold it back, as I always do.

Antosh is back in my mind now, his grimace, his evil stare, cutting through me like a dagger. 'You don't belong here,' he says in a strangely calm voice, as if it is the one thing he is saying not just for the sake of hurting me, but also because he knows it is true. I know it is true. I know I don't belong there. I know I don't belong anywhere. I never have done and I never will. I hold back more tears with all my might.

Antosh disappears into thin air, as Alice had done and I am left standing on my own in the catering corridor of my old high school. I think to myself that I should be happy, I should feel safe, I should be grateful he has gone, but all I feel is broken and alone. I want someone to appear, anyone, even Antosh was a distraction from the person who hurts me most of all.

I can't take the silence any longer. It's deafening. 'You don't belong. You don't belong. You don't belong.' I run along the corridor seeing bloodstains on the shining tiles as I pass. I don't know if they are mine at the hands of Antosh that terrible day in year nine, or my parents, or Eric or Bernard. Or maybe, I think to myself, as a shudder comes over me, they are mine from something that is yet to come.

I slam through the doors at the end of the catering corridor and run out into the place that was usually densely populated with teachers but today there is nobody around, just me. 'Just me.' I'm so scared and alone. I sprint as fast as I can through the school and out the doors to the playground.

It is empty, but I can hear all the noises that I would do if it were packed. The screaming, the chanting, the laughter that I'm convinced is directed at me. Heading straight for the opening in the shrubbery and the rotten fence, I feel as though people are chasing me. I don't know if it is Antosh, if it is anyone else or if it is my demons.

I reach the fence.

Without even stopping to feel the security of the shrubbery, which now seems more like the ideal place to be cornered than a place of safety, I put my foot straight on one of the holes in the wood and clasp my hand around the top. I'm somehow back at my year nine height, so the fence is quite difficult to climb. I feel weak and frail, but my determination helps lift me up onto the top of it.

I pause for a moment on top of it. The noise from the playground behind me still rages in the background; my demons still scream in the back of my mind, but as I look out into the open field, stretching up the hill and into the distance, and my eyes fix on the withered willow tree, I feel an ounce of peace, the smallest imaginable ounce.

Then I jump down off the fence and fall into the bush below. I close my eyes as its thorns and sticks ruck up my trouser legs and scratch my shins and my hands.

Then, I open my eyes to look into the distance as I did all those years ago. I still feel like the notion of peace is out there somewhere waiting for me, the idea of belonging. I know deep down that it is not, but for some unknown reason I still feel it; and looking into the distance makes me think it might be more than just an irrational feeling. But, as I open my eyes from the bush I'm lying in, I am horrified to see in front of me not the grass stretching out and up the seemingly everlasting hill, but a white wall, five feet in front of me as high as the sky and stretching out left and right into both horizons.

I climb out of the thorny bush, blood dripping from my legs and hands and I start to smash desperately against the wall with all the strength I have left after a life time of desperate and impossible searching. As I bang against the wall, my blood pours out and streams of the purest red I have ever seen start falling down the white and onto the grass I'm standing on.

I become weaker and weaker and more and more tired and more and more hopeless with every smash against the wall, until I eventually, after what seems like an eternity, fall to the ground in a puddle of my own blood, a puddle of my desperation and close my eyes in exhaustion.

I can't see the wall through my shut eyelids, all I can see is darkness, and I don't have the energy to open them, but I know I don't need to. I know that there is nothing to see. I can sense the wall right there next to me, the wall that marks the edge of my world, a world in which I don't fit inside; the wall that symbolises the story of my life.

Just to make a hundred percent sure that it is still standing in my way, even though I am certain I am too old and weak, laying there to do anything even if it wasn't, I reach out an exhausted arm to touch it.

It is still there, and its surface is as hard and smooth as ever.

As soon as I touch it, I hear a sudden frantic and overwhelming noise and a beeping all around me and I open my eyes.

Back I am then on the train.

We've just stopped at Southwark. I don't know if I had been asleep or not but if I wasn't, I was so deep in my imagination I hadn't even noticed the last few stops.

The train doors are beginning to close. I'm as awake as ever now. I feel like I'm aware of everything going on around me, all the noises, all the people, all the books that the people are either reading or pretending to read.

The doors close.

I'm thinking about how they slammed shut and blocked out the inside of the train from the outside completely in a split second, a complete divide, a complete cut.

I'm having a thought.

The train starts moving again towards London Bridge.

I'm thinking about how the glass barriers are about seven foot high that stand between the platform and the track at London Bridge station, and how they open in perfect unison with the doors of the train to let passengers off. They are there to prevent desperate people from committing suicide.

For some people, there is no escape in this world. For some people, the white walls around them stretch high into the sky and out into every horizon. Even if the sea is everlasting and the fields roll out far into the distance, they are still untouchable – unreachable. Even if the moon rises as darkness falls overhead and the crisp air around them is lit with a safe and glowing light, they still feel as if they are in the middle of a battlefield. For some people, there is no escape, apart from one.

I remember my first few months back in London after my year at Belet and how I would always wake up early before my alarm when it was still dark outside and I would look out of my window at the roads below, watch the car lights going past, the lampposts shining down, lining the streets and the lights from the offices spreading out into the distance.

I would wait for the sun to rise from behind an apartment block and as it did, I would almost believe I was still sitting on the rocking chair outside the shed on the vineyard. It filled me with a natural sense of peace and solitude, just the idea of the birds tweeting and the breeze from the vast open fields on my face; but I knew deep down, as I did even back then, that the sunrise over St John's Wood was no different from the Sunrise over Belet.

I had spent my life searching for belonging. Not a day has ever gone by where I haven't prayed that I would one day find somewhere, but all my hopes have long ago evaporated out of my mind into the air that fills the cage I stay trapped in.

As the years rolled by, my lack of belonging caused an unimaginable guilt to grow inside me, as it felt no different to betrayal, as I watched my children grow up with loving but somewhat vacant eyes.

But it wasn't my fault and despite the years and years of blame and self-hatred, I know in my heart that I have never chosen to be the way I am. I have always wanted to be happy; I have always wanted to feel I belong.

The glass barriers are seven feet high. The fence at my secondary school was also seven feet high and I climbed that with ease. I'm taller now, but then again, I'm an old man now. I have no strength and no energy. Although I think I have just enough for one last climb; one last leap.

I'd put one foot on the glass and one hand on the top and I'd propel myself up so that both hands were on the top of it and then it would be easy. In one smooth motion I could be standing on the top, the platform behind me, the track in front of me.

I didn't pause on top of my secondary school fence, I just leapt over desperately without even looking at where I was going to land, but even in those brief few moments, I had the feeling inside me that the prison of life lay behind me and freedom lay in front. Unbeknown to me back then, there was no such thing in this caged world as freedom as it always seems to be waiting just at the end of the next horizon.

But this would be freedom; the second I let myself fall from the other side of the glass barrier onto the tracks below.

I would stand there on the quiet tracks knowing, knowing that true freedom was near, knowing that even if I had never in my life found belonging, I would at least now no longer feel that I don't belong.

Would I really be missed? Am I even the man I pretend I am anyway? Or is it some imposter living in my body with a wife, children and grandchildren with my mind, the mind of that twelve year old boy desperate to escape the bullying and that twenty-five year old man desperate to find his place in this world trapped inside his head, constantly begging to be let free, but keeping quiet for not even knowing where freedom would be.

Is it really me who my loved ones have ever really loved? Is it really me who has ever even loved the ones I've thought I've loved?

I would see the headlights of the train coming from the dark tunnel of the tracks and as they grew nearer and nearer, they would light up every crevice of my broken mind, illuminate every dark crater of my worn out body. The darkness of my days would be over and the light of freedom, the light of happiness, the light of belonging would surround me;

At last.

And I would happily step right into it.

A slight rumbling of the train jolts me back quite suddenly into reality as it slows out of the dark and into the bright light of London Bridge Station.

It stops and the doors open.